ZARIK

CONQUERED WORLD: BOOK TWELVE

ELIN WYN

CLOCK
WALK
PUBLISHING

MIRI

"The toxin will be even stronger than what those bastards have been using on us," I heard someone say.

I thrashed. The shadows in the blackness shifted. My body exploded with pain. Against my cheek was something sharp, maybe even spiky, but not at all durable. A crunching noise penetrated that awful ringing. An earthy smell invaded my senses.

The ringing sound began to dull, but it was replaced by an equally awful rushing in my ears. Something brushed against my cheek. My face twitched. Even that ached. My eyelids fluttered painfully.

I realized I wasn't in a sea of blackness at all. My eyes were closed to protect themselves from the blinding white light that surrounded me. At least I could trust my body to look after itself when I clearly couldn't.

Slowly, I opened my eyes. It was a slow and painful process.

Why did I hurt so much?

The white light was blinding at first, but, as my eyes adjusted, I began to see distinct shapes within the blaze. Pale greens and yellows. A few scratching blinks revealed those shapes to be leaves and branches. I was in the forest.

What was I doing in the forest?

I tried to think back to what happened before I woke up here. Panic seized me when I searched for memories but found nothing but emptiness. It was as if I hadn't existed before this very moment.

I sucked a shuddering, dust-filled breath into my lungs. The air burned my throat. Coughs rattled my body so hard I feared my ribs would break.

Water. I needed water.

I gasped softly. I remembered what water was. That was something. Not much, but it was a sign that my mind wasn't completely blank.

As I lay there, I took inventory of the things I knew for certain. I was in a forest. There was dirt and dead leaves beneath me. Branches and verdant leaves above me. I assumed there were rocks and roots as well.

I needed to see more, see what else I remembered. I

sucked in another breath and willed my body to work. Sharp, brittle leaves dug into my palms as I pushed myself up. Every joint and muscle cried out in protest.

Nausea rolled through me. The hollowness in my stomach told me there was nothing to retch up even if I'd wanted to.

My arms trembled under the weight of my upper body. I still couldn't get my legs to move.

I told myself my situation wasn't as dire as it had been a moment ago. I could see, I could breathe. My movement was limited, but at least I could move.

It occurred to me that I might have a broken bone somewhere. Ah, I could add bones to my list. And blood.

I breathed a small sigh of relief. Things were coming back to me. I just had to think about them for a moment. With great effort, I rolled myself onto my back and supported my upper body with my forearms. They ached and trembled, but I now had a better vantage point of the world around me.

I looked at my legs. I was wearing pants, a thick, durable fabric with a choppy pattern that looked like it was modeled after the forest floor. There was an insignia on one of the side pockets, but I didn't recognize it.

Covering my torso was a different fabric, still durable, but lighter in weight. It was deep blue. Another insignia was sewn into the sleeve. I didn't recognize that one either. The boots on my feet were scuffed from use and worn in certain spots.

Looking at the articles of clothing I wore, I didn't think they belonged to me. Just by looking at them, I could tell they didn't fit right.

The pants were too big. The shirt was tight around my shoulders. The boots looked big to me, but I wouldn't be able to tell for certain until I got up and moved around. Who knew when that would be?

Not I.

I slowly rotated one foot, testing for pain. There was muscle soreness, but nothing unbearable. I rotated the other foot with the same results.

Ankle, muscle, sprain. I knew what those words meant.

I bent my legs at the knee and tried to push my weight onto my heels, but my body wasn't ready to cooperate. It was worn out. I looked around for a good place to rest. I didn't fancy lying back down on the forest floor.

Nearby was a thick tree trunk covered in soft-looking moss that looked ideal. Relying on my arms more than anything, I pulled myself over to the tree trunk. I sat with my back against the moss. It wasn't as soft as it looked, but it stopped the jagged tree bark from cutting into my sore back.

"Okay," I sighed and sharply drew in a breath. My own voice caught me off guard. I forgot I could speak. My throat was dry and scratchy, but I tried to speak again. "Let's try to think about this."

All around me was the forest. It would've been too lucky if there was some kind of sign nearby. But if there had been a sign, would I have been able to read it? Would I recognize the name?

My mouth dropped open in horror as I came to a realization. Could I remember my own name?

No.

What was I going to do if I didn't know my own name? No one would be able to help me if I couldn't tell them who I was.

I closed my eyes. Shutting out the world around me might help me think.

I pictured my own face, an initially difficult task. I knew my hair was dark. I had the strange sense that it was long, but when I reached up and touched it, I found it cropped at the chin. I moved on to the shape of my face. My cheeks felt gaunt. My lips were dry but full in shape. My nose was straight and unremarkable.

I couldn't remember what color my eyes were.

A sea of faces that might've had my features swam through my mind. I flipped through them like an old picture book. A memory slipped in between the fabricated faces. A reflection in a cracked mirror. It was me. I looked scared. The rest of the memory fragments clicked into place. I'd just broken the mirror by accident. The mirror was important for some reason. Perhaps it was very old. My mother was going to be furious when she found out.

"Miri!" The voice in the memory shouted just before the memory faded away completely.

Miri.

That was my name.

Probably.

"Miri." I tested the syllables as if that would give me some kind of confirmation.

What now?

I remembered the forest as a vast and dangerous place. I assumed the odds of someone stumbling across me here were slim. I stood a better chance if I somehow figured out where I was and going from there.

I closed my eyes again, hoping to call up another useful half-memory. I saw flashes of a city street. For a split second, I smelled fried johnnycakes from a street vendor. I squeezed my eyes shut tighter in an attempt to bring the memory into clearer focus.

I saw the wrinkled face of the street vendor. He smiled and thrust a johnnycake into my unexpecting hands. I tried to give him money, but he refused.

The johnnycake was sweeter than I expected. The vendor must've glazed it with honey.

This memory was pleasant, but not helpful. It faded away like smoke before I could think of anything useful. Surely I knew the name of that city. I clearly knew the street vendor.

A name struggled to take form on my lips.

Kluster. No, that wasn't right. Kanter. No.

Kaster.

The name clicked into place with the memory. That street vendor was from Kaster. Was I from Kaster?

I tried to dig up another memory, but nothing came up. All I knew for sure was that at some point, I'd made friends with a street vendor in Kaster. But where was Kaster?

I squeezed my eyes shut and concentrated until pressure throbbed between my eyes. Looking for my locked memories felt like trying to empty an ocean with a cracked bucket.

Another name surfaced after some time.

Duvest. I was pretty sure it was another city. Was it near Kaster? More importantly, was I near either of those places? Even if my memory was perfectly intact, figuring out where I was would be a challenge. Nothing in my surroundings gave me a clue.

With a long, tired sigh, I let my head rest against the tree trunk. I decided I wasn't going to worry about where I was right now. Until I started to remember more, there wasn't much I could do. Besides, my body was exhausted. Whatever had happened to me had taken a serious toll.

Perhaps I simply needed some sleep. My eyelids were already drooping.

Yes, just a few moments of sleep and I would wake up feeling much better.

Right?

ZARIK

Do you know what one of the biggest benefits is to essentially being invisible?

You basically get to do what you want without getting into too much trouble for it.

The other big benefit?

People say things around you they normally wouldn't because they don't remember or notice that you're there.

In my case, being invisible had its advantages before the *Vengeance* was destroyed. I used to collect things, things that most of the rest of the crew thought were unusual, disgusting, or downright weird.

And that was fine. I enjoyed my collection, and my solitude. It wasn't like I had earned or deserved people's attention.

Now, before the ship blew up, I was Zarik—second engineer. Rouhr had brought me on board and given me an opportunity to prove myself and regain my honor.

Another one of the benefits of no one ever paying attention to you was that you generally heard many things that wouldn't normally be said while you were around.

Such as—today, when I had been walking behind General Rouhr, Strike Team Commander Karzin, Strike Team Commander Sk'lar, and two of the human guards, they were speaking of a woman that had come in earlier that day, distressed about her missing daughter.

Curious, I followed Karzin and Sk'lar as they headed out to the room where the woman was, ready to file a missing person report.

With a datapad in his hand, Karzin looked more bored than interested in the whole situation.

"Mind if I join you?" I asked them right before we stepped inside the cramped interrogation room. Sk'lar looked back at me over his shoulder, eyebrows shooting up as if only now he was realizing I had been following him, and exchanged a glance with Karzin before shrugging.

"Suit yourself," he said. "This is probably nothing."

Following him, I stepped inside the room and took a

seat across from the middle-aged woman. She had deep wrinkles around her eyes, wrinkles that seemed even deeper in her distress, and a few streaks of white hair had already started to take over her brown hair. In a room that was nothing but three bare walls and a one-way mirror, she looked even smaller in stature than she really was.

"Finally," she cried, nervously running her tongue over her lips. "I've been waiting here for almost an hour."

"I'm sorry, ma'am," Karzin said, his tone polite. "Busy day."

"I understand that, but I'd like to see some effort being put into looking for my daughter."

"Ma'am, I can assure you...the city officials are already doing the best they—"

"That's bullshit," she cut him short, her lips tightly pursed. "I know they haven't even looked for her outside the city, or even in the ruins. That's why I've come here. I need *your* help."

"Very well," Karzin sighed, flipping his pad open and readying for some notes. "What can you tell me about your daughters? And when was the last time you saw her?"

His stylus flew across the datapad quickly as the woman spoke, but just one glance at the pad and I could see he wasn't taking notes of everything.

Just the basics, the outline.

That was unlike him.

Karzin had always prided himself on a job well done, so I never thought he'd be the kind of commander to do things in a lackadaisical manner.

"Right, I think we have everything we need," he finally said when the woman was done with her story. "I'll see what we can do about it, and we'll be in touch."

"Thank you," she breathed out, looking more relieved now. As for me, my curiosity had turned into perplexity. The moment Karzin, Sk'lar, and I left the room, I couldn't help but stop them.

"What was that about?"

"What do you mean?"

"You didn't seem particularly concerned in there," I replied, doing my best not to accuse them of negligence. "Almost as if you didn't believe her."

"It's not that," Karzin shrugged. "Do you have any idea how many missing reports I've had to file these past few weeks? Communication between cities is spotty at best, and the war has brought on mass migration. Most people have just up and left without telling their families about it."

His jaw tightened. I knew, we all knew, how he felt about family. About losing family. This had be harder on him than I realized.

He took a deep breath and continued. "Some see it

as an opportunity for a fresh start, or they just want to run away from it all. The way I see it, this woman's daughter just got a new job somewhere and left to do it. I've noticed that many of these humans don't even speak to their family for many days, even though they are in the same place. This girl has probably just gone off and forgotten to say something about it. We shouldn't waste the resources."

Sk'lar, surprisingly, had been inclined to agree with Karzin...not about the girl's lack of compassion and common sense to speak to her mother, but about not wasting resources looking for her.

That wasn't a huge surprise. K'ver in general were known for their logic. And Sk'lar, in particular, had a reputation for putting practical concerns first.

And last.

"We have enough to deal with handling these anti-alien factions that are spreading their filth around the city and other towns. I say we send one or two people out to look for her for a day, then go back to dealing with what is right in front of our faces. If this is a problem, surely the human guards can take care of it."

"Understood," I agreed and merely nodded, already thinking.

Predictably, the general listened, but disagreed.

The two human guards, both lieutenants for the city if I read their rank insignia correctly, disagreed with one another. One of the them, the fat one, agreed with Karzin and Sk'lar. The other felt that it was our duty to investigate.

It was the other one that I agreed with.

And still, it wasn't my place to say anything.

Yet.

I went down to my room and sat, hunched at my desk. Despite Tobias' efforts to find me a proper chair, he had been unable to find one that allowed for my considerable height.

However, discomfort did not bother me.

It was merely something to be endured.

I quickly got into the database and began my search for the file that the city officials had undoubtedly created. As surly as Karzin still was, despite his connection to a human female, he was a stickler for files.

Even if he'd decided that there was little we could do, I was betting he'd have found the report by the city officials and attached it to his own.

He created and kept files about everything. And, as I'd suspected, there was a file about the missing woman.

Opening the file, I read the report, which was detailed, and wondered how he could simply throw this situation to the wayside.

Perhaps he'd found the report, but not bothered to read it. It was the only explanation.

The woman in question had strong ties to the city. She had been a volunteer in the cleanup process, as well as at one of the local food banks.

None of her neighbors, co-workers, or friends remembered anything about her saying that she would be leaving. According to statements taken by the city guard that had investigated, she had left the city only three times during her life, and one of those was during the invasion.

As a matter of fact, the last she had been seen by anyone was on Seyka Street heading to her work.

How could Karzin possibly feel that this woman had simply taken a new job somewhere, or had just gone somewhere without telling her mother or her friends?

They must have merely looked at the beginning of the file when the mother came in and assumed things.

Very well, if they were unwilling to look into this, then I would.

It wouldn't be wasting valuable resources.

I wasn't a resource. I was invisible. Unnoticed.

Most importantly, perhaps this would be a way for me to begin to restoring my honor.

And for that, I'd do anything.

MIRI

I stumbled through the forest in a daze, tree
branches whipping my arms with every step I took.
With no idea of where I was going, I didn't even know
if I was venturing out of the forest or further into it, but
I didn't even care.

All I knew was that I had to keep walking.

Easier said than done, of course. I was growing
weaker with each passing minute, my stomach
rumbling audibly: I was so hungry that I could eat the
bark off a tree. I stopped for a minute then, one hand
on a tree trunk as I tried to catch my breath.

My body was soaked with sweat, locks of greasy
hair plastered on my forehead, and my muscles felt as
heavy as lead.

"Yes, please," I muttered under my breath, noticing

an overgrown thorny bush just a few feet away from me. Red berries weighed down its thin branches, and I landed on my knees as I started picking them eagerly. I stopped when I had a handful, my hands shaking from how weak I was, but I hesitated before putting any of the berries into my mouth.

Were the berries even edible? Or could they be poisonous?

I tried to rack my brains for an answer, but there was nothing. Either I had never known about wild berries, or I simply couldn't remember. "Great," I groaned, opening my hand and allowing the berries to spill onto the ground.

I watched them roll away from me with a heavy heart, and for a moment I even thought of taking the risk and eating them anyway.

I didn't. As hungry as I was, I didn't want to risk poisoning myself and possibly a slow painful death in the middle of nowhere.

Groaning, I pushed myself up to my feet and dusted my pants off. I scanned my surroundings once more, praying for my memories to return, but I found nothing but the echo of my own thoughts inside my head.

The only thing I had was a name—Miri—but that was as useful as a good behavior badge during trench warfare. In fact, I would be much happier if I didn't know my name and, instead, knew how to distinguish edible berries from poisonous ones.

"Just keep walking," I told myself, frowning at the sound of my own voice. It sounded strange and familiar at the same time, which made for a really unsettling experience.

I decided to keep my mouth shut as I walked, knowing that it'd be of no use to obsess about who I was...or used to be. The important thing was to find a way back into civilization. If I had any luck, there'd be some kind of city or town nearby.

Of course, I could also be stranded in the middle of nowhere, no other human being for miles in each direction.

Thankfully, it just took me a couple of hours before I stumbled on what seemed like a small outpost. Still a few hundred feet away from its outer walls, the thick vegetation keeping me hidden from sight, I took a moment to examine it.

The walls were small despite their sturdy appearance, and I could see a dozen squat buildings right behind them. There didn't seem to be much activity going on, but it was better than nothing.

Only when I started walking toward the outpost did I realize there were guards posted on the main gate. There were just two of them, and they were casually talking between themselves, their guns holstered. Even though I didn't like the idea of talking with someone that could potentially shoot, I had no other choice but to keep on walking toward them. They had already seen me, after all, and one of them was even pointing his finger straight at me.

"Good morning," one of them greeted me, and I was about to reply when I noticed there was something odd about them.

Not just odd.

Wrong.

They were much taller than a regular human, and their muscular bodies looked as if they had been designed to intimidate.

They wore full body armor that almost entirely covered their skin with secondary plates.

Wait.

That wasn't body armor.

That was their skin.

And it was *green*.

These weren't humans...they were aliens.

I froze in place, not knowing what to think, and the two guards exchanged a confused glance. They started walking toward me and I couldn't stop myself from panicking.

"Stand back!" I cried out.

Where the hell was I? And why were freaking aliens here?

I knew there was an answer for those questions buried deep in my mind, but I couldn't dig it out fast enough. Especially with two green and scary-looking giants making their way toward me.

"Calm down, miss," they continued to say, their deep voices making my heart beat even faster. Could I even trust them?

I was still trying to calm myself down when I realized they were walking away from each other, trying to flank me. They seemed hesitant about me, and that definitely didn't make me relax.

Before I even knew what I was doing, I had already launched myself forward and was running past them. They called after me, but that just made me run even faster, my feet kicking dust off the ground as I went.

I dashed into the small outpost in a panic, but I breathed out with relief as I realized there were humans inside the walls. A few threw curious glances my way, but most of them didn't even pay me any attention and just carried on with their normal lives.

"Come back here, miss!" The alien guards shouted from behind me. Looking back over my shoulder, I realized they were closing in on me and I decided to keep running.

No way was I going to let those two lay their hands on me, that was for sure. I was still glancing back at them, clearly not paying enough attention to what was in front of me, when I hit something and tumbled to the ground.

"Crap," I groaned, wincing as pain shot up from my knee to my thigh. There was a small overturned cart in front of me, a few jars of herbs and spices littering the ground, and all of it seemed to belong to a small elderly woman that was looking at me with an expression of pure confusion.

"What's wrong with you?" One of the guards frowned, the two of them now looking down on me. Great, I had been caught. "Why the hell are you running away from us?"

"Because...you're aliens?" I tried, not sure what else they were expecting me to say.

"So?" one of them asked.

"She's probably a member of an anti-alien group," the other scoffed, folding his arms over his chest as he eyed me disapprovingly.

"I don't even know what you're talking about," I said meekly, looking at the elderly woman beside me and hoping for some support.

Her eyes jumped from me to the aliens, and then went back to me again. She seemed as confused as I and the aliens were.

"Do you know this woman, Kanna?" the guard closest to me asked the old woman. She shook her head and pursed her lips, her eyes never leaving mine.

Slowly, she went down on one knee and offered me a smile, locks of white hair tumbling over her shoulders.

"My name's Kanna," she said gently. "I'm this settlement's herbalist. Do you have a name?"

"Miri," I replied.

"Good. And how can we help you, Miri? You look a lil' bit lost, if I may say so," she continued, the kindness on her voice enough to make me feel more at ease. "Where have you come from?"

"The woods," I said, quickly glancing back to the place where I had just come from. Frowning, Kanna just eyed me for a short moment, her focus on the small cuts and bruises on my arms.

"And before the woods?"

"I... I don't know," I admitted, feeling a knot in my throat. Why couldn't I remember anything? There were so many questions bouncing around inside my head, and I felt that the answers were there, too...but somehow, they remained beyond my grasp. "I don't remember anything."

"You don't remember?" one of the guards asked, both his eyebrows arched.

"I don't. I just remember running through the woods..."

"Alright, sweetie," Kanna said, rising to her feet and offering me her hand. I took it, allowing the old woman to help me up. "Come with me into my shop, will you?

I'll get you something to eat and drink, and these two gentlemen will try to figure something out."

I was too confused to protest. The aliens didn't seem hostile, and even Kanna seemed to trust them.

Besides, the important thing was that she had offered me food. At that point, I was hungry enough to follow whoever promised me a handful of breadcrumbs.

"And what are we supposed to do?" one of the guards asked Kanna, both of them looking uncomfortable. They seemed more prepared to deal with situations that required the use of a gun than with mysterious girls that didn't remember absolutely anything.

"Don't you have superiors?" Kanna told them sternly. "Get one of them on those comms of yours and tell them what's going on. There has to be someone in the city capable of helping her."

"Right," one of them said, clearing his throat. "Of course."

"Now, let me just pick these things up and we'll go," she started, bending over to pick the jars of herbs I had knocked over. I helped her do it, feeling embarrassed about the whole situation, and then we were on our way.

"Those two aren't the smartest of them," she said as we left the guards behind. "But they mean well."

"Yes, but..."

"But?"

"They are aliens!" I said, keeping my voice low so that no one could hear us.

"Why, of course they are," Kanna laughed. "Where have you been living all this time? Under a rock?"

"I have absolutely no idea," I said.

And that was the truth.

ZARIK

I was in the process of modifying a separate datapad to look even deeper into missing persons reports when I got a ping on my primary.

There was a report of a girl that had been found, complaining of memory loss.

If I could help this young girl, that would be a step in the right direction to redeem my honor.

To redeem myself.

And maybe, just maybe, I could become something other than a nameless shadow in the general's ranks.

Heading out of my room, I made my way straight to the general's office. As usual, nobody paid me any heed as I strolled through the maze of corridors.

I hesitated for a second as I stood before the

general's door, but then sucked in a deep breath and rapped my knuckles against it.

"Come in," he called, and I stepped inside the office, careful to keep my back straight and my posture perfect. I saluted the general and he gave me a slight nod. "At ease. What brings you here, Zarik?"

"Sir, I was made aware of a situation in a nearby settlement, and I'd like to help out."

He narrowed his eyes at me, almost as if he was weighing each one of my words, and then he drummed his fingers against the desk's surface. Pushing the stack of reports he was reading to the side, he gave me his full attention.

"A situation, huh? What are we talking about here?"

"Apparently a girl has been found close by, and she is suffering from memory loss. There might be a connection to a missing person case I've come across. I think you're aware of it, as well, sir."

"I am," he sighed. "A common occurrence these days, unfortunately. But I don't get it. Why the sudden interest in this situation, Zarik?"

"I want to help this girl recover her memory, and that means that I want to help her," I explained.

He sat back and folded his arms over his chest. He was bewildered by my offer. "Why you?"

I threw my hands in the air and started pacing his

office. "You know why, sir," I said. "You know that I need to atone for what happened in my past, and this is a step in that direction. Please, sir. You have to let me help this woman."

He shook his head. "And that's the reason why I shouldn't let you go. You're trying to use this for your own advantage instead of legitimately helping this young lady."

"No, sir," I said. I was frustrated. How could I show him that I deserved to do this?

"I admit that this request is a bit selfish, but I honestly wish to help her. I may not have an understanding of what life is like when you lose your memory, but I do know what it is like to have your life turned upside down. That makes me uniquely equipped to help her."

He shook his head. "You've always taken that job too hard to heart. You made a mistake, and it's something you're going to have to live with, but it's not something that defines who you are. Trust me, I've made many mistakes that have led to people's deaths."

He uncrossed his arms, stood up, and walked up to me. "You can't let it define you. If you do, you'll end up doing something rash, like hacking into a secure system and using that information to get yourself a mission."

Oh.

I put my head down. "My apologies, sir." Then, I picked up my head and looked him in the eye. "But I don't regret my decision. I can do this, sir."

He sighed. "You know, I was planning on sending one of the teams to go get her," he said.

"Why would you do that, sir?" I asked. "Isn't that overkill?"

"What do you mean?"

I saw his grin, but answered his question nonetheless. "You would be sending five fully-armed, fully-trained commandos to go pick up one girl with memory loss. Imagine how confused she would be, how scared she would be, and how bad that would look. How long do you think it would take for her, or anyone else, to start thinking that she was some sort of criminal?"

I had to give him credit for holding back his smile. "I hadn't thought of it that way," he lied. He had to have lied. There was no way my explanation actually worked. "But, what if there's someone, or some number, of the anti-alien group around and they decide to get hostile?"

I looked at him like he had lost his mind, if only for a brief second.

"Sir. Really? I have had training while in your service. While I'm not as highly trained as the strike teams, you know that I can handle a weapon. Besides, look at me," I said as I stepped back, giving him full view of the improved me. "I'm not exactly defenseless."

He graced me with a nod. "Okay."

"I'm sorry?"

He nodded again. "I said, okay. The job is yours. I'll give you the location and you can go get her. Make sure you're prepared, just in case."

"Thank you, sir," I said. I couldn't believe he was letting me do this. I turned to leave.

"Zarik?" he asked.

"Yes, General?" I asked, swinging back around.

"You'll be taking the rift," he added.

"Yes, sir."

He shook his head and dismissed me. I quickly went back to my quarters, put on my body armor that I used in place of my scales, and gathered my electronics and my personal weapon, an oversized double-barreled blaster.

I went to the armory to get some additional ammunition and a go-pack - a small pack with rations and an emergency shelter and other emergency supplies - and went outside the office, waiting for Rouhr to order the rift for me.

He sent me the location coordinates, ordered the rift, and wished me luck.

As the rift opened, I felt a bit of excitement that I hadn't felt in quite some time.

And maybe, just maybe, something like hope.

MIRI

"I don't know how to thank you," I said, drinking the rest of the soup from my bowl. Now that I had a full stomach, I felt like a completely new person.

Which was funny, since I didn't know what my 'old self' would have felt like.

My strength had returned, and I was no longer feeling dizzy and disoriented. Sure, my memories still hadn't returned, but it was a start.

"No need to thank me, dear," Kanna smiled, placing a cup of tea on the table. Steam rose from it toward the ceiling, but I went for it and took a small sip anyway. It had a sweet taste, and I closed my eyes and let out a small moan. "These days, it's important we look after each other."

"I wish more people were as kind as you are," I told

her, not entirely sure if my words had anything to do with my past or if they were just a generic statement. Either way, it was still the truth—there could never be too much kindness in the world.

Sitting by the table in Kanna's small store, I rested my elbows on it and peered out the small bay windows. The two guards from before were just standing around in front of the store, and they threw me casual glances from time to time. I was no longer afraid of them, but I wasn't entirely sure what to make of the fact that aliens were now a reality.

A reality that everyone else seemed comfortable with, even took for granted.

When exactly had that happened?

"You really don't remember anything, do you?" Kanna asked me, sitting opposite me, watching as I studied the strange green men.

Not little green men, that's for sure. I choked on my tea.

She took a sip out of her own teacup, leaning back in her chair as she waited for me to reply. When I didn't, she offered me a small smile and decided to continue. "What about the Xathi? Does that word ring a bell?"

"Xathi?" I echoed, looking down at my hands as I turned the word around inside my mind. The word was familiar, yes, but at the same time it was a completely meaningless one. I had no idea what a Xathi was, or why it was important for me to know that. "Is that a city?"

"Not a city, I'm afraid," she said patiently, shaking her head slightly. "Valorni? Skotan? Puppet Master? Do you recognize any of those words?"

"Not a single one," I sighed, blowing the rising steam off my tea. "It's like...I can *feel* the answers to all those questions, just like you can feel your body growing hot or cold...but I just can't seem to grab any of them. They just seem to slip away from me."

"Well, don't strain yourself, dear," she smiled. "Someone will be able to help you, you'll see."

"Someone? But who?"

"I think the answer to that has just arrived," she smiled, jutting her chin to point toward the windows. I followed that direction with my gaze just in time to see an alien appear right in front of the store. And there was no better way to describe what had just happened than that. There was a blinding light for a moment, as if a doorway into another dimension had just opened, and then the alien materialized out of nowhere.

He was muscular, more than the two outpost guards, and there wasn't a single hair on his head. His skin was completely white, except for slight tinges of red, and he struck a more imposing figure than the aliens from before. It seemed that he was their superior:

the guards saluted him almost right away, and then they started speaking in what seemed like a formal tone. I couldn't hear what they were saying, but I was pretty sure they were talking about me.

Nodding to the guards, the white alien then turned on his heels and started heading toward Kanna's small store. My heart started beating anxiously, but Kanna didn't seem too concerned with the newcomer. Apparently, to have aliens pop out of nowhere in the middle of the street was a normal occurrence.

"Is this Kanna's?" the alien asked, scanning the inside of the room. He had a stern expression, one that almost made me want to shrink and disappear, and he was even taller than I had thought. If he wanted to, he could pick me up and tear me in half without breaking a sweat.

"Yes, it is," Kanna nodded. "I'm Kanna. Are you here because of—"

"I am," he cut her short, his eyes now focused on me. He had acquired his target, it seemed. "I came to pick her up."

"Very well," Kanna continued, getting to her feet slowly. "She has already eaten, but you must get her to a doctor. As I'm sure the guards have told you, she's suffering from memory loss and—"

"I'm aware," he grunted. I wasn't sure if the aliens

had any special abilities but, if they had, small talk was definitely not on the list.

"My name's Zarik," he introduced himself, stopping just a few feet away from where I was sitting. He was so tall that I felt as if I had a skyscraper in front of me. "Please come with me."

I hesitated, not sure if I should trust him. Perhaps feeling my anxiety, Kanna laid one hand on my shoulder and tried to soothe me. "It's okay, sweetheart," she said. "They might look mean, but they're real softies when you get to know them."

Zarik raised one eyebrow at that but didn't say a word. Apparently he wasn't too keen on being described like that.

On that, we agreed: if I had to describe him, 'soft' would definitely not be one of the adjectives I would use.

"Okay," I finally said, pushing my chair back and standing up. As if on cue, the alien turned around and started walking out of the store. Not knowing what else to do, I thanked Kanna hurriedly once more and followed after Zarik.

"Have you ever used a rift for travel?" he asked me, and only then did I notice he was pointing at what seemed like a portal. It was right there on the street, light streaming out of it, but no one really seemed to pay any attention to it.

"No, I haven't," I admitted, already dreading the experience. "At least, I don't think so."

Did he really expect me to walk through that thing? I felt the palms of my hands grow damp with sweat and, for a moment, I considered making a run for it. Was I really going to trust this guy?

In the end, though, he didn't give me a choice.

"It's not hard," he said, laying one hand on my shoulder and guiding me forward. "It is not, technically, painful."

I stumbled through the portal with him.

It felt as if I had dived headfirst into ice water.

My nerve endings came alive with the shock and, even though the experience didn't hurt, it still left me completely disoriented.

So, yeah, not technically painful was accurate.

Still not something I was looking forward to repeating.

In the blink of an eye, I had left the small outpost and now I was standing inside a building. Zarik and I were in a small room that was almost completely bare, but we didn't stay there long: the moment we stepped out of the portal, he marched out of the room and then down a long hallway. I trailed after him, my eyes growing wide as I saw even more aliens roaming the corridors of the building I was in.

Green, hulking ones, with purple stripes. Gray-skinned ones with ... circuitry embedded in their skin?

Broad, tall ones that looked a little like Zarik, except they were all shades of red. None were like him, not exactly.

And that probably wasn't the top of my list of concerns right now.

Maybe all the ghost-white aliens were in another building.

Having a party.

"Where are we going?" I asked Zarik, trying to get my thoughts back under control, but he said nothing. Either he hadn't heard me or he simply didn't care about me. I thought about repeating my question, but decided against it and remained quiet.

At the end of the hallway, Zarik made a sharp left turn and stepped inside what looked like a doctor's office. There was a large desk in the center of the room, and a small stretcher bed to the side of it; one of the walls was covered with tall cabinets, but another was lined with tables filled with medical equipment I didn't recognize.

Sitting behind the desk was a woman wearing a doctor's white coat. She smiled the moment she saw Zarik walk through the door, but her expression turned into one of concern the moment she laid eyes on me.

"This is Dr. Evie Parr," Zarik announced. "She's going to fix you."

ZARIK

"Let's keep calling you Miri for now, alright?" A pretty name. And I hadn't thought to ask her.

She nodded, eyes wide and worried, but Dr. Parr continued. "If you don't object, I'd like to run a couple of scans of your brain to see if there is any kind of damage or anything else we can discover," Dr. Parr said. "I'll run the results by one of our resident brain experts for a second opinion before I come back to you."

"Okay," Miri said hesitantly. I could see that she was nervous, but Dr. Parr was fantastic at helping people feel comfortable.

Even me.

Miri ran her hands through her hair. It was very dark, cut roughly along the same line as her chin.

Many of the women here had short hair, but hers looked choppy, almost as if it had been cut in a hurry. Was that the intended style?

She was pretty by human standards. A bit too skinny, but pretty.

I had learned to look at the human females differently after many of our crew had begun to get into relationships with them.

This young lady, Miri if I had heard her name correctly, was pretty. She had bright eyes and full lips that I found appealing, and her light-colored skin was similar to my own.

"It's okay," Dr. Parr said with a smile. "Nothing is going to hurt, and Zarik will be here the entire time."

That didn't seem to comfort her much. Seeing Miri's look, Dr. Parr looked at me. "Did you not treat her nicely?"

Ah.

"Unfortunately, Dr. Parr, I may not have been focused on politeness and protocol," I admitted. I actually did feel bad. I'd been focused on the first step of my mission: retrieving her, bringing her back to the hospital so that she could be reunited with her family.

Manners had fallen by the wayside.

Regret must have been clear in my tone, because Miri cocked her head, looking at me differently than she had before.

Dr. Parr shook her head. "You know better, Zarik." She turned back to Miri. "He'll be nice, I promise. If he's not, then tell me and I'll kick his ass for you, okay?" Dr. Parr's easy smile seemed to relax Miri, because she smiled in return and nodded.

"Good," Dr. Parr said with a nod. "Now, let's get you all set up for the scans. If you could lie down on the table?"

Over the next few minutes, Dr. Parr positioned and repositioned Miri however was needed for the scans, then when she was finished, she told us that she was going to go take a look at the results. She would be back soon.

There was an awkward silence in the room for a bit after the doctor left. Miri didn't look at me much, and I tried not to look like I was staring at her. I did notice that she had a jagged scar on her right arm.

I wondered where she had gotten it from.

"I, ahem," I croaked, trying to clear my throat. "My apologies," I said as I cleared my throat again.

She gave me a perfunctory smile. It was more than I deserved.

"I wish to apologize," I started, "for my earlier behavior. I was rude and inconsiderate."

"Why?"

I looked at her and found myself staring at her eyes. They were a bright golden brown and seemed to be filled with loss and pain. I suddenly found myself wanting to take that loss and pain on myself just so she would feel better.

I opened my mouth to answer, but was unsure of what I should say. I wasn't sure if I should tell her the truth - that I was trying to help her to redeem my own past mistakes - or if I should tell her that I was trying to help because I understood the patronizing sympathy she would face as someone without her memory.

"I meant, why are you apologizing?" she asked. "It's not like I'm someone important. Am I?"

"I don't know," I answered. "You know more about who you are than I do," I said.

"Not like that's saying much," she remarked. Then she looked up at me and seemed to study me. When our eyes locked, I wasn't sure what I saw in her look, but I found myself hopeful that she wasn't disappointed. "But, why are you apologizing?"

"You deserved better treatment from me," I said. "I... I am not normally rude towards people. It's not generally within my nature."

"Then why were you rude towards me?"

I shook my head as I shrugged. "I haven't had as much contact with humans as my crewmates have had. Among my people, the Skotan, niceties are not always universally prized, especially soldiers fighting a galactic war against an oppressive foe. I failed to tailor my approach to you."

"I see," she said. Then she looked at me nicely. "Thank you for apologizing. At least you're being polite now."

I nodded. Before I could say anything more, Dr. Parr came back into the room.

"That was fast," Miri said.

"I got lucky that our resident brain specialist was already in the building," Dr. Parr responded. "Dr. Daphne March has the most experience with the effects on the brain that some of our local issues have caused, so I had her look over the scans with me to verify what I was already seeing."

I could tell by the tone of Dr. Parr's voice that Miri's brain scans troubled her. Local issues could probably only mean one thing.

"What is it, doc?" Miri asked.

Dr. Parr smiled. "Call me Evie. As for your scans, they're clean."

"Clean? What does that mean?"

Dr. Parr took a seat next on the exam table next to Miri. "What it means is that, structurally, your brain is fine. There's no damage to the tissue. Now, that's a good thing," she said quickly. "But, the downside is that it also means we don't know what caused your memory loss. What we're getting from you doesn't match up with any of the scans from the people that were affected by the Puppet Master."

"Puppet Master?" Miri asked.

"Oh," Dr. Parr blinked. "There's been some contact with vines that have a memory inhibiting gas," she summarized. "We've tried to make a detailed study of the people who were affected, how their neurons behaved."

"Right." Miri shook her head. "Just one of those things I need to catch up on."

Dr. Parr nodded sympathetically. "I'm afraid so."

"So...I'm confused," Miri said. "Not just about the memory altering vines, but if my scans don't match the other people, then what about any of this is a good thing?"

Dr. Parr smiled. "It's a good thing that your brain is healthy and fine. It's a good thing that, if you weren't attacked by the...vines, we can rule that out." She shrugged. "Sometimes that's half of what medicine is."

"Okay."

"However, what that may mean is that you were dosed with something, and that is the troubling part," Dr. Parr explained. "If you were given something, or exposed to something, it's new. We don't recognize it at all."

"So, again...how is any of this a good thing?" Miri

questioned again. I had to agree with her. I was confused, as well.

"Given how your synapses are reacting on the scans, Dr. March and I suspect that you don't have permanent memory loss," Evie said. "That's a good thing. Whatever is causing your current memory issues is probably temporary."

She tapped her fingers on the desk before her. "I could give you some of the serum we used on the people that were affected by the Puppet Master's memory-loss gas. It might help, it might not, but it's harmless if it turns out to be ineffective."

Miri looked at me, seemingly lost. "I...guess so, doc. I mean, if it helps me get my memory back, I'll try it."

"Okay. Give me a few minutes, okay?" Dr. Parr said, a smile still on her face. "We'll help you, I promise. Okay?"

Miri only nodded.

I wasn't terribly excited, though. She was still going to be without her memories, and that didn't seem to be right.

From an entirely selfish standpoint, if I turned her over to the city officials for them to help, I had still done a good thing and that was at least a start to fixing my lost honor.

But it seemed wrong to just drop her case off with someone else. The best course of action for me, but mostly for her, would be to help her regain her lost memories. It was something that I would have appreciated if I had been in the same situation.

I needed to help this woman. She deserved it.

I just had no idea how to go about doing so.

How do I help someone regain their memories when no one knows how she lost them?

MIRI

I liked Dr. Parr. She had a way of making the most catastrophic event seem like it was an easy fix so long as everyone kept a smile on and was willing to put in some elbow grease. I almost forgot that my memory loss posed serious medical concerns, that's how calming and effective Dr. Parr was.

"Is there somewhere I can take you for you to recover?" Dr. Parr asked with a kind smile. Before I could tell her no, the Skotan who'd rescued me stepped in.

"That won't be necessary," he answered.

I was momentarily grateful that I didn't have to admit I couldn't remember where I lived or even who I knew.

"She should stay here in the medical wing so her progress can be monitored," the Skotan said.

Wait, what?

"I would've liked to be asked, Zarik." Dr. Parr narrowed her eyes, though her smile never wavered.

"As would I," I quietly chimed in.

"Do you have a bed to spare, Dr. Parr?" Zarik asked.

"As it happens, I do," Dr. Parr replied.

Zarik turned to me.

"Is there another place you'd rather be?" he asked. I shook my head, feeling out of control and kind of pathetic. "Then there's no problem." His grin was charming, but there was something behind his eyes I couldn't identify.

Something hard.

I looked away before he could catch me staring. I had no right to be critical of him after all he'd done for me.

"There's no problem," Dr. Parr said. "Now that you've assumed the role of her primary guardian, can I talk to you for a moment?"

"I'm her what?" Zarik sputtered.

"It's on your orders that she's remaining here. I need someone to call if there's an emergency." She quickly turned to me with a reassuring smile. "Not that I'm anticipating one. Aside from your memory, you're in perfect health. Or at least you will be once we get some food in you."

"Right." I pulled the hospital blanket up to hide my embarrassingly thin body. Wherever I'd been, there clearly hadn't been enough food.

"I'll have some brought up from the dining hall," Zarik added.

"It's called a cafeteria when we aren't on a ship," Dr. Parr corrected.

"Is it a big room with food and tables?" Zarik replied.

"Yes," Dr. Parr nodded.

"Then it doesn't matter what we call it."

"Talk. Now." Dr. Parr put her hand on his pale shoulder and pushed. Zarik rolled his eyes but did as he was told. They didn't go far, just to the other side of the room. They tried to talk in hushed voices, but that didn't stop me from hearing every word.

"Can't you tell me anything else about her?" Dr. Parr asked.

"How would I know anything? I was simply sent to retrieve her," Zarik replied.

"All right. Fine. I'm sure you've already worked out that the dose I gave her has a pretty low chance of reversing her memory loss," Dr. Parr continued.

I frowned. I had agreed to take the medicine with

the assurance that it wouldn't have any negative side effects, not that it wouldn't have any effect at all.

"Then why did you try it?" Zarik asked.

"I can't think of anything else. There are no signs of head trauma or brain damage," Dr. Parr answered. "Do you know of anything else causing spontaneous amnesia besides the Puppet Master?"

"Too much ale and a serving of bad swampfish?" he smirked.

I let out a small, quiet chuckle. I didn't want them to know I was listening. I assumed Dr. Parr wasn't saying all of this to me directly in a kindhearted attempt to not overwhelm me.

"This is serious," Dr. Parr replied. "I'm going to give her another brain scan in a few hours. We'll know for sure if she was exposed to the Puppet Master."

"I hope for the general's sake that it's something else," Zarik said somberly. "If it was, that truce is as good as over."

I didn't have a clue what the Puppet Master was. Dr. Parr had said something about vines, but that made no sense. The name alone made me uncomfortable. I decided I wasn't ready to find out more about it until Dr. Parr confirmed that it did something to my brain.

"Let's not jump to any conclusions yet," Dr. Parr warned Zarik. "Right now, let's work together to help this poor girl."

Zarik looked over at me. I looked away, but not quickly enough. He knew I'd been watching them. He probably guessed that I'd heard everything they said.

When I risked another glance, he was still looking my way. Dr. Parr was saying something, but he clearly wasn't listening, and neither was I.

When Dr. Parr said something that required an answer, Zarik finally looked away. A strange chill skittered over my skin that wasn't entirely unpleasant. I pulled my blanket tighter around my shoulders. I looked down at my bony wrists and frowned. A little food would be nice right about now.

As if by magic, an alien carrying a covered tray entered the room and set it down by my bedside.

"What's this?" I asked with a grin.

"Bedside service straight from the dining hall." Zarik walked over with a grin, clearly pleased with himself.

"When did you order that?" The smells coming from the tray were mouthwatering.

"I punched it in on my comm unit." He took off the tray lid with a flourish. A cloud of steam rose and curled in the air for a moment before disappearing. The tray held a variety of small dishes, most of them containing some kind of meat. I eyed the slice of chocolate cake.

"Eat slowly," Dr. Parr advised. I looked at her like she was crazy. How could she expect me to slowly work my way through this buffet of delicacies? "Trust me. You haven't had proper nutrition in who knows how long. I'm sure you want to stuff your face, but the moment you do, you're going to throw it all back up."

"Oh," I said quietly. "Yeah, I don't want that."

"Try the soup first," Zarik suggested. "It's easiest on the stomach. Work your way up to the filet and chocolate cake.

"The chocolate cake is what I wanted to eat first," I laughed.

"I could tell," Zarik smirked. "You looked at it like it was the love of your life."

"At this point, I'd say it is," I joked. Zarik's laugh was low and rumbling. The sound made me want to smile, so I did.

"It seems like you're feeling better," Zarik commented.

"Considering the state you found me in, I'd say anything afterward has been an improvement," I replied.

I picked up the spoon and scooped up a generous mouthful of soup. It was thick with vegetables and meat. The moment the warm, savory broth touched my tongue, I let out a moan and closed my eyes. Zarik laughed.

"I take it you like the soup," he said. I nodded and took in another large spoonful.

"Pace yourself," Dr. Parr warned once more.

"I'm trying, but it's hard," I said between mouthfuls.

"Should I take the soup away, Doctor?" Zarik asked.

I brandished the spoon at him. "Careful, I'm armed," I grumbled.

"Well, she's certainly got spunk and a sense of humor," Dr. Parr laughed. "Both of those will come in handy as we figure out what happened to you."

I tried to smile at Dr. Parr, but some of that delicious soup went down the wrong pipe. I let out a sputtering cough and gasped for air.

"Okay, I'm taking this away from you now." Zarik whisked the soup out of reach while I chugged the glass of water on the tray.

"It's clearly for your own safety," Zarik said when I gave him a withering glare. "And you're not as scary as you think you are. The hospital bed doesn't exactly give you a menacing air."

"I've got some reports to file," Dr. Parr announced. She put a gentle hand on my shoulder. "Hit the button next to your bed if you need me for anything."

"Thank you," I replied. When Dr. Parr left, I turned to Zarik. "Thank you, too."

"Oh, I'm not a doctor," Zarik replied. I furrowed my brow.

"I know. But you're the one who brought me here," I

explained. "You also brought me food and made me laugh. You didn't have to do either of those things."

Zarik didn't say anything. He opened his mouth like he was going to speak, then he closed it again.

"You don't have to say anything if you don't want to," I shrugged. "I just wanted you to know that I'm grateful to you. You saved my life."

He looked me in the eyes then. His expression wavered between bewilderment and something much softer that I couldn't name.

Maybe I didn't remember the name for that expression. However, I could see that he was fighting something inside him.

I didn't know much about the alien races that now lived on my planet, but the ones we'd passed on our way to Dr. Parr's office had seemed strangely militaristic. Expressing emotions might not be part of their culture or they didn't do it the same way humans did.

Not wanting to make him uncomfortable, I just smiled.

"Did I butter you up enough to give me my soup back?" I asked.

He lips turned up, just a bit, as he handed me back the bowl.

ZARIK

"I'd like to schedule an appointment with General Rouhr," I told the young human secretary, Tobias. With a quick smile, he tapped his keyboard a few times and only then did he look up to me.

"A reason for the appointment?"

"It's about the human female I retrieved. The general is aware of the situation."

"Very well," he nodded curtly. A few more taps on his keyboard, his eyes taking in whatever was on his computer screen, and then he gave me a bright smile. "You're in luck. The general has a short opening in about twenty minutes. Will that work?"

"Yes. I'll wait here."

Taking a seat in an adjoining room, I tried to stop my mind from wandering as I waited. The situation with Miri was fragile, and I wanted to make sure I handled it perfectly.

If I wanted to regain my honor, I couldn't fail at this job, especially after practically begging the general to let me handle it.

And Miri...she trusted me. Maybe.

As promised, Tobias came to get me after twenty minutes. With his polite smile and professional posture, he led me toward the general's office and pushed the door open for me. Tobias had become the general's right hand, but I had never gotten close to him the way other members of the strike teams had.

"Zarik." General Rouhr sat up straighter when he saw me. "I wasn't expecting you this morning. Did Tobias leave you waiting long?"

"No, sir," I replied. "I wanted to keep you abreast of the situation with Miri -- the human female."

"Is there anything to report?" General Rouhr asked.

"She's with Dr. Parr. We're monitoring her brain activity to see how her interaction with the Puppet Master's serum affects her."

"You don't sound thrilled," General Rouhr said with a slight smirk.

"I'm pleased that the human female will be kept here for observation," I replied. "However, the potential cause of her memory loss doesn't sit easily with me."

"Oh?" General Rouhr asked.

"Sir, taking recent events into consideration, you must admit it's suspicious," I prompted.

"Do you know for certain that our new ally is involved?" General Rouhr asked.

"No," I admitted after a pause.

"Then let's not jump to conclusions just yet," the general advised.

"Yes, sir." I wanted to ask him what else he thought could cause such complete memory loss, but I held my tongue.

"I'm surprised at you." General Rouhr leaned back in his chair, folding his arms over his chest. "It's not like you to take such a personal interest in a case."

"In fairness, this is the first case involving other people I've worked on in a while," I reminded him. I'd been confined to engine rooms and workspaces, toiling away under the watchful, yet idiotic, Thribb.

"I would've taken you out of the engineering position long ago if I suspected you were going to handle it so well," General Rouhr replied.

There wasn't much about my situation that I liked.

Being the disgrace of the crew was not a position anyone would envy. However, General Rouhr always gave credit where credit was due and I respected him for it.

"If I didn't handle it well, Miri would be completely alone," I replied. "I couldn't walk away. I'm determined to see this through until she can remember what happened to her."

"That's very honorable of you," General Rouhr replied. The word honorable sent a zing through my body.

"I'll leave you to your work." I nodded and ducked out of the office. I didn't want the general to see my grin. However, my grin faltered when I thought of the human woman in my care.

She'd placed her trust in me, believing my intentions to be selfless. That wasn't the case. When I first accepted this case, I saw her only as a way to regain my lost honor. I hadn't expected Miri's situation to be so intense.

There was no true reason why I couldn't help her but also help myself.

If she got the care she needed, then where was the harm in me taking advantage of the situation to better my own life?

I was tired of tinkering with circuits in my out-of-the-way work areas. I longed to be back in action, doing what I was trained to do.

And who was Miri to me, really? She and I were strangers, despite the fact that she trusted me. It made no sense that she had the ability to swirl up guilt within me. I wasn't lying to her, I wasn't causing her harm.

There was no reason for me to feel guilty.

None at all.

Telling Miri that I took her case to help my situation wouldn't do her any good, but it also wouldn't do her any harm.

There was no reason for her to know.

With a firm shake of my head, I pushed away the nonsensical guilt. I tried to ignore the kernel of it that remained when I returned to my room. Sitting behind my desk, I turned on my old computer terminal and immediately got to work.

I wasn't sure if more people like Miri had found their way into a government database, but I was going to find out.

Karzin insisted that the city officials log everything properly into the system, and that meant pretty much everything of interest that happened ended up in the system.

I started by going over the missing persons database once more, and I cross-referenced it with the clinical files from the hospital.

I hoped to find a link between cases of memory loss and persons that might have been missing, but finding a connection proved harder than I expected. Either I was looking at the problem the wrong way, or there simply wasn't a connection to be made.

But there had to be.

I was sure of it.

There had been a spike in the number of missing persons, and that was shortly after contact with the Puppet Master was made.

I knew Karzin believed that was nothing but a coincidence, and that most people simply up and left, looking for better pastures, but I was pretty sure there was something else going on.

After all, Miri wasn't a case of skipping town to look for a better job. There was something nefarious about her whole situation. Problem was, I couldn't seem to figure out what it was.

After a couple of hours of staring at the computer screen, I finally called it quits. I pinched the bridge of my nose for a second, took a deep breath, and finally rose to my feet. Maybe if I saw Miri, I'd manage to get something out of her.

Leaving the room, I made my way to the hospital as quickly as I could. Always a busy place to be, I somehow managed to make my way into Miri's room without having anyone stop me.

One deep breath and I stepped in.

"How is everything?" I asked, forcing an easy smile to my face.

Miri smiled faintly when she saw me. The tension that lingered in her eyes melted away.

She really did trust me.

It had been so long since someone looked at me

with something other than doubt or outright malice.

I grabbed a chair and placed it next to her bed. Part of her blanket was twisted. Out of habit, I reached to fix it. Years of military training had instilled the desire to have everything neat and just so.

My finger brushed against the back of her hand. Her skin was colder than I expected it to be. I looked at her. My concern must've been obvious in my expression.

"My hands are always cold," Miri shrugged. "It's nothing to worry about."

"Humans are supposed to be able to warm every part of their bodies automatically," I frowned.

"Human bodies prioritize what needs to be warmed the most. Hands are low on that list," Miri replied.

My instinct was to cover her hands with my own, but I restrained myself. I didn't want to startle her with sudden contact.

She stared up at me. I stared back. I couldn't speak, my brain couldn't come up with anything to say. Eventually, I offered her a smile. When she smiled back, I felt something in me soften.

"Tests are back!"

Dr. Parr burst into the room. I retracted my hand and tore my gaze from her face.

"What can you tell us?" I asked.

Us.

Miri and I weren't an us. I had to be more careful

with my words.

Dr. Parr addressed Miri.

"The dose I gave you earlier had a positive effect on your brain," Dr. Parr smiled.

"That's good." Miri looked from Dr. Parr to me. Her hopeful expression faded when she looked at me. I was scowling. "Isn't that good?"

"It means that you were exposed to the Puppet Master's memory-erasing gas," I informed her.

Her eyes filled with worry. "What does that mean?"

"She might've been in one of the cities that was initially attacked," Dr. Parr said to me.

"Do you have a way to check?" I asked.

"I kept records," Dr. Parr replied. "I'll go look through them." She gave Miri one more reassuring smile before leaving us.

"That can't be good," Miri sighed.

"Why do you say that?"

"Because neither of you answered my question and then you started talking about me as if I weren't here," she said.

"Dr. Parr and I don't want to cause unnecessary alarm." Miri gave a dry laugh.

"I woke up in the forest with no memory and a new scar. There isn't much you can tell me that will cause more alarm than that," she said.

Well, that was likely true.

"When you put it that way," I chuckled. "A few months ago, some human settlements were attacked. At the time, no one could figure out what was doing it. The attacker left minimal clues behind and none of the people who were present remembered anything."

"You think I could've been there?" she asked. "With those vines you mentioned before?"

"You've been exposed to the memory-erasing gas, so it's likely," I answered.

"But you said that was months ago." Her eyes widened with fear. "That would mean I've been wandering around for months doing who knows what! How could I have survived that?"

"You're more resilient than you think," I told her.

"It still doesn't seem possible," she insisted.

"All that matters is that you survived it," I replied. "You don't have to ask why you survived it. It'll drive you crazy wondering why you survived something you probably shouldn't have."

"Sounds like you know what you're talking about," she prompted.

I froze. I didn't want to bring up my past. If I did, I'd have to tell Miri about the disgrace that followed.

"I'm a soldier. Almost everyone in this building is a soldier. I'd say we all know what we're talking about on that front," I said smoothly.

"I suppose so," Miri agreed.

We sat in silence for a few moments. Since I spent most of my time in solitude, I was used to silence. Usually, when there was a silence between two people, there was pressure to fill it. I didn't feel that pressure. Miri seemed content to sit quietly. I wondered what she was thinking about.

I was almost disappointed when Dr. Parr returned.

"I'm sure," she nodded. "At least as sure as I can be. The records are a complete mess right now. Some have been lost during the war, some databases aren't fully operational, and God knows what other issues the war has caused."

"I see." The doctor was right. The war had wreaked havoc on the planet's administrative system, and it'd be a few years before everything was running smoothly again.

Still, I knew that a large quantity of records had survived the war. Apparently, some people did remember to make backups. "Did you run her fingerprints?"

"Yes, and not only that." Smiling patiently, almost as if she was talking to a concerned parent, she continued. "I also took a DNA sample and tried to find a match on all available databases, but there was nothing. No match when it comes to facial recognition, either."

"That's odd."

"Not really," she shrugged. "Most surviving database

and record indexes have to do with criminal records, and unless she was a criminal before…"

"Understood," I breathed out. Even though it was frustrating, I couldn't help but feel happy with the knowledge that Miri wasn't a criminal. At least as far as the surviving records indicated.

"But if you want, you can check the records yourself," Dr. Parr offered.

"No," I sighed. "I'll take your word for it."

"If I wasn't there, then where was I?" Miri's voice wobbled as she spoke.

"We're going to figure that out." I laid a hand on her arm. "I'm not giving up. Dr. Parr isn't giving up. Are you going to give up?"

Miri shook her head.

"Then it's only a matter of time before we unravel this mystery." My smile concealed my troubled thoughts.

If Miri hadn't been caught up in the early attacks, that must mean the Puppet Master had attacked something we didn't know about.

When the reports had filtered down, I had been skeptical about the news about the Puppet Master.

General Rouhr and the others might be convinced, but I wasn't ready to believe the Puppet Master was a gentle giant.

Too much had happened to allow me to believe that.

MIRI

When Zarik entered my hospital room the next day, I was in the middle of the muscle strengthening stretches Dr. Parr had showed me how to do. Already, I was feeling much better and stronger, though I still needed to gain back some weight.

I smiled when he came in, but my smile vanished when I saw his face. He looked agitated. There was a small wrinkle between his eyes where his brow furrowed.

"Is everything all right?" I asked from my bent over position. I was trying to touch my toes without bending my knees. It wasn't going well. I straightened up slowly and then turned around to face Zarik, who looked less agitated now. In fact, he looked a little dazed. His eyes roved over my body, which was fairly exposed in the hospital gown I wore.

Dr. Parr had brought me a change of clothes a few hours before, but I hadn't planned on changing until after I completed my stretches.

"Zarik?" I prompted. His eyes locked on mine for a moment, before he shook his head and went back to scowling.

"I'd like for you to speak with the general," he said.

Now it was my turn to scowl.

"Why?" I asked. "I mean, I'm happy to, but I still don't remember very much. I don't think I'll be of any help."

"Don't worry about that." His voice suddenly went soft. He placed his hand on my shoulder, giving it a gentle squeeze. His hand was so large, my shoulder was completely covered by his palm. I could feel the warmth radiating from him.

I fought the urge to step closer.

I looked up at him and gave him a reassuring nod.

"Let me change first, okay?" I asked. "I don't want to meet your boss in hospital rags."

"That's a good idea," he nodded. "I'll be waiting just over here." He pointed to the door.

I walked back to my bed and closed the privacy curtain. The clothing laid out before me was going to be big on me, but it looked comfortable.

I pulled on the pair of soft black leggings and the plain white shirt that fell to my mid-thigh. I briefly wondered whose clothes these were. I guessed they belonged to Dr. Parr. I made a mental note to thank her later.

Dr. Parr had set the shoes I'd been wearing before to the side of the bed. They looked clumsy and awkward now. I didn't have another option, and I certainly wasn't going to meet the general barefoot, so I pulled them on. They were a bit big.

"Okay, I'm ready." I threw back the privacy curtain. Zarik gave me another long look.

"You look comfortable," he said finally.

"I am," I grinned.

"You're in a good mood." As I passed him, he put his hand on the small of my back to guide me in the direction of the door.

"Staying in the hospital was boring," I shrugged.

As we walked through the corridors, he kept his hand lightly touching my back. We received odd stares. I wasn't sure why. I was grateful for his guiding hand. I definitely would've gotten hopelessly lost if I had to navigate through this place on my own.

Again, the halls were filled with aliens and humans. Evie had explained to me, reminded me, I guess, that the green guys were Valorni, the few gray ones were K'ver.

And the red ones with scales were Skotans. She'd blushed just a bit at that, and I had to wonder why.

But no time for that now, as Zarik knocked on General Rouhr's door. A deep voice bid us to enter. When we stepped in, a red alien looked up from his desk. I realized he was a Skotan, same as Zarik. But Zarik's skin was white, only red in some places.

I thought back to the aliens I'd seen in passing. Nope. Not a single other Skotan with that coloring before.

Was it rude to ask about the color of their skin?

General Rouhr looked surprised to see me, but quickly rose to greet me.

Was this meeting not his idea?

Hell. That couldn't be good.

"General Rouhr, this is Miri," Zarik gestured between me and the general.

"Nice to meet you." I felt like I should bow. Was I supposed to bow? I had no idea. Even with my memory intact, I wouldn't know how to address different military ranks.

"It's an honor," General Rouhr dipped his head. I mimicked the gesture. "Though I must confess, I'm not sure why you're here. Shouldn't she be in the hospital wing receiving treatment?"

"That's the thing, sir," Zarik replied. "Dr. Parr ran

some tests and we found out Miri was exposed to the memory-erasing gas secreted by the Puppet Master."

"She was in one of the settlements that were attacked?" the general asked.

"No," Zarik clarified. "She wasn't."

"That is deeply concerning news," he said thoughtfully. "Whatever happened to you, Miri, I'm sorry. But I don't think we should discard our alliance with the Puppet Master just yet."

"Why not?" Zarik demanded. "It attacked her recently. How can you be sure it didn't say whatever you wanted to hear so that nothing stood in its way as it took over the planet?"

Up until that point, I'd assumed the Puppet Master was a person. But they kept referring to it as an it. And they said it wanted to take over the planet. That didn't sound like something a single person could do. For the first time since Zarik brought me here, I felt unsafe.

"I spoke to it. Several members of the crew spoke to it. It was sensible. I would even call it kind. Are you telling me you doubt my judgment?" General Rouhr fixed Zarik with a dark look that made me take a step back.

"No, sir," Zarik replied, uncowed. "I just wasn't sure if you had all the available facts at your disposal."

There was a long silence, while the general considered.

"It's ridiculous to speculate without adequate information, when the answers are readily available. We are going to the home of the Puppet Master," General Rouhr declared.

"I don't think that's wise," Zarik blurted. "We could be walking into a trap."

"I've given the Puppet Master my trust. You know as well as anyone that my trust is not easily won. In fact, you know that better than most," General Rouhr replied.

I looked up at Zarik, wondering what the general meant. Zarik's face was hard and expressionless. Clearly, General Rouhr had struck a nerve. I wanted to ask, but I held my tongue.

"And don't think I'd be so foolish as to do so without insurance. You know me better than that." the general smiled wryly as he pulled out his comm unit.

He motioned for us to follow him. Zarik's hand found its place to my back once more as we moved through the crowded corridors in the general's wake.

He led us to an open foyer with a high ceiling. Within minutes, several large, well-armed aliens of different species approached us. They said nothing but there wasn't a doubt in my mind that every single one of them was capable of killing me in multiple ways.

"Will this do, Zarik?" the general asked. He gave me a reassuring smile.

"This will do fine," Zarik agreed.

"We'll keep the rift open in case something goes wrong," the general added. "If something does go wrong, your only job is to get Miri to safety."

"Miri's coming?" Zarik asked. "She shouldn't be put at risk."

"She's the one at the center of all this," General Rouhr replied. "Perhaps the Puppet Master can help her."

"Your optimism is inspiring." I didn't miss the note of sarcasm in Zarik's voice. "Shouldn't Miri be given a say in the matter?" He looked down at me with a small smile.

"Yes, I think I should," I spoke up.

"Very well," the general asked. "Miri, are you willing to meet the Puppet Master?"

"That depends," I replied. "What *is* the Puppet Master?"

"It's difficult to explain." General Rouhr rubbed the back of his neck. "Think of the Puppet Master as the heart of the planet."

"I don't understand." My brow furrowed.

"I know," the general replied. "Like I said, it's hard to explain. It's far easier to explain once you meet it. It's fond of human females."

I gave the general a curious look.

"Oh, no, not in that way," the general assured me. "A

human female was the first one to make contact with it. I think it likes the gentle nature of the human females it's met so far."

"Better not send Leena down to meet it," one of the soldiers called out, and another one, one of the large green ones, smacked the speaker. Hard.

"I see," I replied even though I still didn't understand. I felt like I was supposed to know what General Rouhr meant by *that way*, but I couldn't remember.

"If you think it can help me, I'd like to go," I decided.

"At the very least, I think it can provide you with some clarity," the general replied. He lifted his comm unit and spoke to a mechanical sounding voice as he input coordinates.

"You can change your mind at any time," Zarik assured me.

"Good to know."

I watched with wide eyes as a shimmering strip of light again appeared in front of General Rouhr and his troops. The strip widened, almost like a window. But it wasn't the foyer on the other side. It looked like an underground cave.

I watched the general and his troops step through. When it was my turn, I reached for Zarik's hand and held it tight. The first time had been nerve-racking.

Once again, I found myself in an unfamiliar place I didn't understand. We were in an entrance to a large tunnel that descended steeply as we entered a cavern.

I held fast to Zarik's hand, desperate to be near the only thing that made sense.

ZARIK

biting coldness chilled my bones as we stepped into the rift, its embrace already familiar to me. Miri, though, gasped and pressed her body tight against mine. She hadn't used the rift as many times as I had, and she still suffered every time she had to travel through it.

"I'll never get used to this," she muttered the moment our feet found solid ground.

"Yes, you will," I smiled. "Everyone eventually does. It's just a matter of patience."

"If you say so."

She didn't sound convinced, but her focus was now on the large cavern entrance ahead of us. With the general leading the way, we all headed straight into the cavern, its shadows swallowing us whole. We pushed the darkness away with our flashlights, but none of that seemed to make Miri relax. She was tense and on edge, but I wasn't exactly surprised.

A meeting with the Puppet Master would leave anyone on edge.

"Don't worry," I said, trying to calm her. "Everyone says the Puppet Master is actually quite nice once you get to know him." I wasn't sure how I felt about that, but I didn't want her worried any further.

"Him? It's a he?"

"Well, not exactly." Scratching my chin with one hand, I tried to think of a way to explain it. "It's not a 'he', and it's not a 'she'. It's something different."

"I'm not sure if I understand."

"Don't worry," I chuckled. "There's a lot I don't understand, either. We only learned of the Puppet Master a few weeks ago, so this is all new to everyone involved, really. What's important for you to remember is what the general said: the Puppet Master is the heart of the planet."

My words echoed through the cavern complex, and a few of the team members looked back at me, as if my voice was making them nervous. It seemed that it wasn't just Miri who was on edge. To be fair, I was a little nervous myself. I had never met the Puppet Master but, going by everyone's reports, I was in for a surreal experience.

"How can anything be the heart of a planet? That just sounds even more confusing." Frowning slightly, she let out a sigh. "I mean, why is it friendly now? Evie's been trying to fill me in. I thought it was fighting us just a few weeks ago, when it trapped the city with a dome of vines."

"That's true," I nodded. "But apparently that was just a knee-jerk reaction of sorts while he was waking up. Sort of. He was trying to look after everyone, and stop more damage from happening." Skrell. Even I didn't sound convinced. Probably because I wasn't.

"And do you think the Puppet Master can help me?"

"Well, we're about to find out, aren't we?"

She said nothing at that and, for a long moment, the only sound echoing throughout the cavern was that of heavy boots stepping on the rocky cavern floor.

Miri's grip tightened on my hand as we moved farther into the cavern, the shadows growing longer and darker all around us. When I glanced down, her knuckles were white. I covered the top of her hand with my other hand and squeezed gently.

"I'm sorry," she gasped. "Am I squeezing too hard?"

"Not for me," I replied. "But your knuckles might feel otherwise."

Miri loosened her grip enough to allow blood to flow back into her hand.

"You've been here before, right?" she asked, casting nervous glances in every direction.

"General Rouhr has. Many of the crew escorting us has. I, personally, have not." I decided to be honest with her, even though that could potentially make her more nervous.

"What's going to happen now?" she asked. "How are we going to talk with the Puppet Master?"

"General Rouhr is going to talk to the Puppet Master. Hopefully, if it's honest, it will tell us if something happened to you."

"What do you mean, if it's honest? Didn't you say you believe General Rouhr, and that the Puppet Master is an ally?" Miri asked. Without giving me a chance to reply, she continued. "But then, yeah, that thing with the dome happened. And it did attack human settlements. This is all a mess." I heard the distress in her voice.

"It's a complicated situation. I haven't provided you with an adequate explanation yet. Mostly because there's a lot I don't know myself, but also because I didn't want to overwhelm you," I explained. "Believe me, I wouldn't have let you come if I thought you weren't going to be properly protected."

"Thank you." She gave my hand another squeeze. That time fear wasn't the motive.

"Keep the rift open." I heard General Rouhr speak into his comm unit to the AI that Fen had set up.

Good. Miri and I would have an easy escape should something go wrong.

"You always have such an intense look on your face," Miri commented. Before I could say anything back, I felt her soft, cool fingers against my cheek. "I suppose intensity is a good trait for the person responsible for my safety to have."

"Intimidation comes in handy more often than combat skills," I replied.

"I wouldn't know anything about that," Miri replied. "Though, I don't know about anything right now. Maybe I do know about stuff like that." She peered up at me. "Do you think I look like someone who knows things about combat?"

I looked her over.

"I don't get that sense from you," I replied. "Even if your mind didn't remember, your muscles would. You'd move differently."

"Then it's doubly good I have someone like you to look out for me." She appeared to be more at ease. I was glad to help her. As I focused on the feel of her hand in mine, I realized that I missed having people rely on me. I wouldn't let her down. I would prove to her, and to everyone here, that I could be trusted to keep a life safe.

I'd make up for my terrible mistakes in the past.

Before I could rein in my thoughts, my mind wandered to the last family I'd been charged with protecting.

The family that never reached their destination.

Because of my failure.

Reality melted away as I heard their screams again.

"This place is amazing," Miri spoke suddenly, dragging me back to the present. I realized I'd been holding my breath. "I didn't know anything like this existed on this planet." She paused and laughed at herself.

"I should stop saying things like that. It's pretty redundant that this point."

"At least you're in good spirits about the situation," I replied.

"I have to laugh about it," she replied. "If I didn't laugh, I'd cry."

"We wouldn't want that, now would we?"

I couldn't take my eyes off her as she took in her surroundings. Suddenly, her eyes went wide.

"What's that?" She pointed with a trembling hand. I followed her gaze. Suspended by thick, ropy vines was what looked like a giant flower bulb.

"That's the Puppet Master," General Rouhr called back to her.

"*I was not expecting you,*" A voice in my mind put me on edge. I'd heard of the Puppet Master's ability to speak into one's consciousness. I hadn't thought to prepare myself for it. From the shocked expression on Miri's face, I could tell she's heard the voice, too.

"I should've warned you about that," I murmured to her.

"That would've been helpful." I looked down at her and saw the glint of humor in her eyes. She was teasing me.

"Next time we meet an ancient telepathic lifeform, I'll be sure to warn you," I teased back.

"There are none like me here," the voice came again.

"Pardon our intrusion," General Rouhr spoke up. "I've received some troubling news concerning your ability to erase memories. I wanted to give you a chance to answer our questions."

"How diplomatic," the Puppet Master replied.

"My goal is to preserve our alliance. We simply want answers," the general explained.

"I will do my best to accommodate you," the Puppet Master agreed.

"We thank you," General Rouhr dipped his head.

"This seems to be going well," Miri whispered to me.

"It's always best to let General Rouhr do the talking," I replied.

"Really? You're much more charming," she whispered back.

"Is that another attempt to make light of the situation?" I asked.

"Partially. That doesn't mean it's not true."

"Thank you." I gave her hand a light squeeze. When I glanced at her, she didn't look as frightened as she had before. I probably didn't need to hold her hand anymore. I considered letting go, but I realized I didn't want to.

"Ask your question," the Puppet Master commanded.

"This human female may have been exposed to your memory-erasing gas. She was not at any of the places you've targeted before. Have you targeted another settlement we didn't know about?"

"No," the Puppet Master answered. *"You know everything I've done."*

I tried to hide my frown.

Of course, the Puppet Master would deny it regardless of the truth. It finally had what it wanted.

Our cooperation, our agreement to restrict some of our activities.

"You haven't used your memory-erasing ability for any other reason?" General Rouhr prompted.

"One week ago, by the way you measure time, one of my vines was attacked," the Puppet Master explained. *"I applied the use of my airborne toxin to dissuade the attackers, in an attempt to avoid causing them bodily harm. It worked. I have not been bothered since."*

General Rouhr and his crew turned to look at Miri. She shrank back from the weight of their gazes.

"There must be something else," I said.

"There is nothing else," the Puppet Master replied.

"How do we know it's telling the truth?" I asked the general. "We're at a clear disadvantage. It could be lying about everything and we'd never be the wiser."

"Are you questioning my judgment?" General Rouhr asked.

"I am simply pointing out that this Puppet Master has implied that Miri was part of the attack on one of its vines," I explained. "Looking at Miri, do you think she's capable of that?"

"She doesn't even know what she's capable of," the general replied. "We have the facts. She was exposed to memory-erasing gas. The Puppet Master secreted gas one week ago. I don't see an alternate explanation."

"Perhaps we should ask the female," the Puppet Master cut in. Once again, all eyes returned to Miri.

"How could I help?" she asked quietly. "I'm telling the truth when I say I don't remember anything, I swear."

She looked up at me with frantic eyes.

"We believe you," I assured her.

"Then why ask me?"

"If she was exposed to my memory-altering abilities, I can undo the damage done," the Puppet Master said. Miri

looked away from me to stare at the massive bulb before us.

"You can give me my memories back?" She asked.

"If it is my toxin you've been exposed to, then yes."

Miri looked delighted for a split second before fear worked its way back into her eyes. She stepped closer to me, her side pressed against my arm.

"How?" she asked.

"I will touch you with one of my many tendrils. The process from that point on is simple," the Puppet Master explained.

"Will it hurt?" Her hand trembled in mine.

"It will be painless, I assure you," the Puppet Master replied. Miri chewed her bottom lip as she considered. She looked up at me once more.

"What do you think?" she asked.

"Do you want your memories back?" I prompted.

"Yes." She nodded. "But what if I remember something bad?"

"Everyone has bad memories," I told her. "After what I've seen, I'm convinced you're brave enough to face them."

"What if I used to be a bad person?" That notion seemed to frighten her more than the prospect of bad memories. "What if I did attack the Puppet Master? What kind of person would do that?"

"One step at a time," I soothed her. "Whatever we

learn, we'll deal with it. There's no point in trying to deal with it before we've learned anything. We'll be here for hours if we try."

"Right," she laughed uneasily. She turned back to face the Puppet Master.

"Are you ready?" it asked.

"As ready as I can be." Miri stood up straighter.

"You'll need to release the hand of your companion," it told her. General Rouhr and the others glanced down at her hand, which was still joined with mine. I didn't miss the odd looks we received. Naturally, none of them could picture me experiencing physical contact with another being, let alone one as lovely and trusting as Miri.

"Oh." Miri's voice faltered. She hesitated a moment before releasing my hand.

"Step forward," the Puppet Master instructed. Miri did as she was told.

She stood ramrod straight as the Puppet Master lifted a thin, green tendril and moved it closer to Miri. I resisted the urge to pull her back to me. Her hands were trembling. She was scared.

General Rouhr must've seen the intent in my eyes for he stepped in front of me. He didn't block my view of her, but it would be harder to get to her now.

A sense of dread filled me as the wispy tendril touched Miri's forehead.

MIRI

y mind lit up.

My eyelids drooped the moment the Puppet Master's small tendril touched my forehead, its touch cold but gentle, and my mind became a canvas which my memories were slowly being painted on.

I remembered how Kanna, the herbalist in the outpost, had taken me in. Then I remembered how I'd stumbled through the woods, completely lost, my body collapsing from exhaustion. Those memories were vivid, and it felt like I was watching a highlight reel of the past few days.

The moment my memories went further back, though, all clarity was gone.

I saw myself running through the woods as a child, laughing as I dipped my feet into a cold stream, but that image vanished just as quickly as it appeared. It was replaced by a feeling of coldness, my body lying on a cold table while fear ran through me. I remembered the street vendor once more, but his features remained a mystery.

I saw that and then some more.

Crystalline insectoid creatures out of a nightmare roaming the wilderness, screams and fire, death and hunger. Aliens rappelling out of shuttles, laser rifles in their hands as they opened fire. Human soldiers joining the fray while civilians ran for cover.

My body started to shake as the memories started coming faster and faster, random images flashing behind my shut eyelids. I took it all in but, at the same time, none of the images held any meaning. I wasn't even sure if those were my memories. They felt distant and impersonal.

I could see, but I was blind.

I gasped as the Puppet Master's tendril finally pulled back, all those images and memories fading away at once. It felt as if high voltage had been running through my brain, and now the cord had been pulled from the power socket. My knees felt weak suddenly, and I would've gone down if Zarik hadn't grabbed me, one of his arms around my waist.

"*Whatever happened to you, Miri, it wasn't caused by me,*" that multilayered voice said, the Puppet Master's thoughts somehow becoming my own. *"Your memory loss was caused by a toxin, one similar to mine, but it didn't come from me. I've managed to reverse the process, but the effects will be delayed."*

"How do you feel, Miri?" Zarik asked me, his voice sending a shiver up my spine. I felt his fingertips on my bare skin, on the slight bare space between my shirt and pants, and that brought me back to reality. Zarik was slowly becoming the anchor of my existence. If it weren't for him, I'd be completely adrift.

"I feel…" I trailed off, not exactly sure how I felt. "I'm a bit nauseous," I admitted, running my tongue over my parched lips, "but I think I'll be fine."

"Can you remember anything?"

"Not much," I shook my head. "Just flashes, random memories, but I don't know what any of it means. Everything's a mess. It's just so confusing." As I spoke, I saw myself as a child once more. Loose memories of laughter and children playing with me bubbled up to the surface, and I held on to those as fiercely as was possible. I remembered a world before war, a world on which no alien had set foot. "I... I think I remember a bit of my childhood. It's not much, but I can feel it all coming back."

"The memories will return," the Puppet Master said, *"but you'll have to be patient. It'll take time."*

"That's a start," Zarik said. "What about the past

week, Miri? Even the slightest detail would help us figure this out."

"No, I've got nothing," I sighed, massaging my temples. I could already feel a headache brewing, the back of my head throbbing with pain. "The past few weeks aren't even a blur...they're a complete blank."

"You mentioned a toxin similar to the gas you use," General Rouhr spoke up, taking one step forward as he looked at the Puppet Master. "Do you know where such a thing might have come from? Could there be another creature like you on the planet?"

The Puppet Master didn't say a word for a couple of heartbeats, almost as if it were thinking. More than just that, it seemed like it was hesitating. *"On this planet, I'm the only one of my kind,"* it finally replied. *"Sentient life has existed for ages, but nothing like me. I stand alone. The answer eludes me, General, for I do not know where such a toxin might have come from."*

"Very well," the general nodded, a formality to the way he spoke. I still didn't understand all the politics involved in this strange situation, but it seemed like the general and the Puppet Master respected each other. Even the general's retinue seemed to look at the Puppet Master with a sense of awe. "I appreciate your cooperation."

"As I appreciate yours," the Puppet Master said, his voice so powerful that it seemed to push out whatever

thoughts I had inside my head. *"We're only as strong as our bond is, General. It is our duty to cooperate."*

"It is, indeed." Turning to me, the general then offered me a benevolent smile. "How do you feel, Miri?"

"Better now," I nodded, the nausea I had felt before quickly fading. As for the headache, that one seemed reluctant to go away.

"We're going to use the rift again," Zarik told me as the general instructed his soldiers to start preparing for our return. "So let me know if you feel too weak for it. I can always arrange for a shuttle to come and pick us up, although that might take a while."

"I... thank you," I whispered, looking up into his eyes. My first impression of him was that he was a brute, but now he was starting to grow on me. Underneath his hard shell, there was kindness. "I'm fine, Zarik. I can make it."

"Perfect," the general said, looking at me approvingly. "Since we still don't have the answers we need, you'll have to remain in our facilities, Miri. I'm sure Dr. Parr will feel more comfortable if we keep you under observation. Besides, we'll expect you to have some answers for us when your memories finally return."

I simply nodded back at the general, fully knowing that I had no other option but to do as I was told. Even though everyone had been kind to me, I still felt everyone's suspicions weighing me down and there was no doubt in my mind about what my status was: I was the general's prisoner.

"We'll sort it out," Zarik promised me as the rift opened, a slit of pure light stretching into a doorway large enough for all of us. "Your memories will return, and then you'll be able to go home."

"You can't promise me that," I found myself saying. "I don't even know if I have a home. I don't even know if there's someone out there looking for me. I might be alone."

"No, you're not," he smiled. "As long as I'm standing, you will never be alone."

With that, we stepped into the rift.

ZARIK

I should've had the common sense to foresee this. Of course, things couldn't stay simple and uncomplicated forever. Miri still trusted me to protect her, but how could I if it went against my duties as a soldier? I couldn't risk the first chance I'd ever had to regain my honor. If I messed this up, I might not get another chance. I couldn't keep living my life like this.

A part of me that I was ashamed of, even then, hoped that Miri was up to something sinister. Then it wouldn't matter that I was lying to her.

Even as I formed the thought, I knew it wasn't true. I refused to believe Miri was capable of something horrible.

When I first found her, she was a blank slate of a person. As I spent time with her, she only became kinder. If she was truly inclined to be a bad person, that would've shown through by now.

For all the time I've spent in seclusion, I liked to think I was a good judge of character. Then again, people often misjudged me, so I could be completely off the mark.

At the end of it all, Miri had not been proven guilty of anything. Still, when we returned from the lair of the Puppet Master, General Rouhr pulled me to the side with a concerned expression.

"You're not going to like this, Zarik, but I feel Miri should remain with us for the time being," he said, and I immediately knew he was sugarcoating things.

"What does that mean, sir? She isn't a prisoner, is she?"

"Not exactly, no." He shook his head and, laying one hand on my shoulder, forced a smile onto his lips. "I'm going to order her to a holding cell, but she won't be a prisoner. She'll be our guest."

"A holding cell? That doesn't seem fair, sir."

"I understand you might have misgivings, but it's just a temporary measure." Lowering his voice, he continued. "Despite the Puppet Master's assistance, there's still a lot we don't know about Miri. And although I have no reason to suspect her of anything, we have to tread carefully, all the same. We don't know who did this to her, and what their motives are. It'll be safer for us, and for Miri, as well, if she remains with us. We'll be able to keep an eye on her, she'll have medical resources at hand, and no harm will come to her."

"If you say so, sir," I nodded, even though I didn't like it one bit. Still, there was no use in going against the general, not to mention that his reasoning was solid. I didn't like to think of Miri in a holding cell, but as long as that was for her own security, I'd be able to stomach it.

"Do you want me to tell her?"

"No, sir, I'll do it."

Saluting, I snapped my heels together and then marched to where Miri was waiting for me. She shifted her weight from her right foot to the left as she saw me walk toward her, and managed a nervous smile.

"What did the general want?" she asked me, a thin layer of anxiety coating her words.

"The general believes it'll be best if you stay with us for the time being. I'll have a holding cell ready for you and—"

"A holding cell?" she repeated, all color leaving her face. Her usually rosy cheeks had now turned pale, and her eyes had widened so much they seemed as if they were about to pop out of their sockets. "I'm going to be thrown into jail? I didn't do anything, Zarik!"

"Listen to me," I told her. Her eyes were wide and

frantic. She wouldn't look in any one place for more than a second or two.

"You are not being accused of anything. This is a precaution. General Rouhr would do this to anyone."

"What's going to happen?" Miri asked.

"I'm going to make sure you're put in the most comfortable cell we have. I'll arrange for a cot, clean blankets, pillows, and some kind of privacy screen to be brought down to you. I'll also stop by the cafeteria and make sure someone brings you enough food."

As she processed my words, her panicked breathing began to slow down to a normal rate.

"Does that sound all right?" I prompted.

"It doesn't sound that bad when you put it that way," Miri nodded.

"It'll be better accommodations than the hospital bed," I assured her. "I know the term holding cell is unsettling. If it makes you feel more at ease, almost all of us on General Rouhr's crew have spent a night or two in a cell."

"What did you get put in a cell for?" A shadow of a smile appeared on her lips.

"Oh, I didn't mean me. I'm a model citizen." I smirked.

"I don't believe you," Miri laughed.

"I might have rigged the unit's food storage tank with a tiny bomb filled with neon smoke," I admitted.

"This was years and years ago. It was the only time I ever did anything like that."

"Who'd you get?" she asked.

"General Rouhr," I chuckled.

"Oh my," she laughed.

"You look like you're feeling better about the holding cell," I commented.

"You made it sound tolerable," she said.

"Follow these crewmembers," I gestured to two K'ver waiting to escort Miri. The panic returned to her eyes. "I'm going to go get everything set up, as comfortable as possible."

"All right," Miri gave me an uncertain nod. "I'll see you soon, right?"

"You will," I promised her.

Securing the amenities that I'd promised Miri was not difficult. I hadn't anticipated having to fill out a detailed incident report for General Rouhr.

When I was the second engineer, Thribb handled all of the reports.

It took me the better part of two hours to finish everything. Annoying

When I completed the report, I was mentally exhausted. I stopped by the cafeteria for a quick meal. I also asked for another plate to be sent down to Miri, as well as a message from me letting her know I'd see her first thing tomorrow. It was late enough that there was a chance she'd be asleep anyway. If I was exhausted, I couldn't imagine how tired she must've been.

The last thing I did was send a message to the night guards at the holding cells asking to be alerted if anything happened to Miri. When I received confirmation that I would, I finally let myself fall asleep.

I was startled awake by the wail of my comm unit. It felt like only a few moments had passed, but when I glanced at the clock, I realized it had been hours. I squinted against the darkness to read the illuminated message. It was an alert for Miri's cell.

I was out of bed and out the door in two strides. I didn't bother getting dressed.

What could be wrong? Miri was nervous about being in a holding cell, I knew that. But I thought I'd done a good job of easing her mind.

It briefly occurred to me that there was a possibility she was trying to escape. If she was, that would mean she was guilty of something. I squashed the thought the moment it formed.

I burst into the guard station, startling the two guards at their post.

"What's happened?" I demanded.

"We aren't sure. It looks like the human female is having some kind of fit," a Valorni explained to me. He stepped aside so I could see the surveillance monitors.

One was fixed on Miri's cell. She was sitting up in bed, though she was stooped over, and it looked like she was pulling her own hair.

"Let me down there this instant," I ordered.

"We can't do that," the other guard, a K'ver, protested.

"Do it or I will make you do it," I growled. I had a few inches of height on both of them. By now, I was surely stronger.

"Fine, but you're taking the heat if we get in trouble," the Valorni scoffed.

I moved through the hall, my vision narrowed in on Miri's door. Her cell wasn't unlocked. I shot a glare at the security camera before turning it off.

They weren't going to help her.

They shouldn't even look at her.

Gripping the door handle, I twisted it until the whole mechanism cracked. The door swung open.

Miri sat on her bed, sobbing hysterically. She hadn't noticed that I just broke into her cell.

"Miri." I hurried to the bed and gripped her wrists. She looked up at me, her eyes red-rimmed and wild.

"Zarik?" Her voice was hoarse.

"What's the matter?" I asked. I slowly lowered her hands away from her hair. When I released her hands, she lurched forward. Her thin arms wrapped around my shoulders. Without thinking, my hands gripped her waist and I pulled her against me.

"Tell me what's wrong," I urged her gently. For a while, she couldn't speak. Her breath came in ragged gasps that shook her whole body. I held her steady until she was able to speak again.

"I remember," she said.

"Remember what?" I asked.

"I remember." Another sob broke through her lips. I placed my hand on the back of her head and placed her head on my chest. I hoped I was doing the right thing. I'd never comforted a distressed female before.

I didn't know the protocol.

Was there such a thing?

I was following my instincts. At least, I didn't appear to make things worse.

"I remember, I remember, I remember," Miri murmured.

"What do you remember?" I prompted. She drew breath as if she was planning to speak, but a pained cry was all that came out.

"All right," I hushed. "You don't have to tell me if it causes you such distress."

"I remember," she whispered.

"I know." I turned to the side and pressed a kiss into her forehead. There was no conscious thought to my motions, it simply felt like what I needed to do. Her brow was damp with sweat and her skin was far too hot.

"Should I let go?" I asked. "I don't want you to overheat."

"Please don't let go," she whimpered.

"If you don't want me to, then I won't," I assured her. Some of her hair was matted against her forehead. I gently pushed it back. Her hair was softer than I expected it to be. I ran my fingers through it once more. To my surprise, Miri's tense muscles began to relax. I kept doing that until I felt her arms slip from around my shoulders.

"Let's get you back into bed," I suggested. I gently helped her lie down. I pulled only one of the blankets over her. Her skin was still too hot.

"Wait," her small voice cracked. "Are you leaving?"

"Not if you don't want me to," I told her.

"I don't want you to."

"Okay," I nodded. "I'll sit with you for as long as you need."

I sat beside her and resumed stroking her hair. She seemed to enjoy the physical contact. I wasn't sure how long we stayed like that, but before too long she began to shiver. I pulled the other blanket over her, but that didn't stop the trembling.

"Are you cold?" I asked.

When I leaned down to touch her, I realized she was silently crying.

Without thinking twice, I pulled back the blankets and slid in beside her. She rolled over, pressing her tear-soaked face into my chest.

"You're all right," I whispered to her.

"Talk to me," she answered in a broken voice. "Tell me something that doesn't have anything to do with any of this, something that makes sense."

Tell her something.

For a moment, my shame was on the tip of my tongue, but I stopped. She didn't need to know that.

Not ever.

I gathered her in my arms.

"When I was a very, very small boy," I whispered to her, "I caught a bad case of Piperian fever."

"What's that?" she sniffled.

"We've eradicated most of the childhood diseases that struck Skotans in the past, but Piperian fever just keeps mutating. Adults shake it off in a week or so. Children," I paused, wondering if this was the best story to tell her, "children usually die."

"That's horrible." Her arms tightened around me, as if she could protect me from a long ago threat.

"True. And any progress we've made on a cure has probably been lost to the devastation of the Xathi." I'd never really thought about that. Maybe the Skotan scientists would have found a cure, if we hadn't had to divert so many resources to survival.

"But my grandmother refused to give up on me. She nursed me and kept me in freezing baths, trying to keep my temperature down."

"You're already so warm," she murmured, relaxing.

"If you'd touched me then, I'm afraid I would have burned you." I ran one finger over her upper arm. Such soft skin. So delicate.

"I survived, but the fever left its mark. Bleached my skin, softened my scales."

Made me a freak. But an alive freak.

"I think it's pretty," she mumbled. "Different."

I stayed awake until the trembling of her shoulders stopped.

When I felt sure she was asleep, I gradually let exhaustion claim me once more.

Pretty.

Huh.

MIRI

I woke up with the sun streaming through the window. It caressed my face softly, its warmth spreading across my skin, and it was enough to make my eyelids flutter open. Sitting up in the bed, I ran one hand through my disheveled hair and took a deep breath. My face felt sore from crying, and my eyes were still bleary and swollen. Had I seen my reflection in the mirror, it would probably have been enough to scare me.

I was about to swing my legs off the bed when my hands bumped against something under the sheets. Or, rather, against some*one*. Turning to the side, I held my breath as I realized that Zarik was lying in bed with me, his bare white chest rising and falling softly. Perhaps unconsciously noticing my stare, he stirred in his sleep and opened his eyes.

"Miri?" he asked me with a whisper, looking around the room as if he didn't remember how he had ended up in bed with me. It didn't take long before he breathed out gently, his confused expression giving way to a more relaxed one as he remembered what had happened the night before. Sitting up, he reached for me and laid his hand on top of mine. "How are you feeling?"

"Much better," I said, reinforcing my reply with a nod. My heart sped up a bit as I felt the touch of his fingers on my hand, his hand so big it made my own feel incredibly tiny. "And all because of you," I continued, not capable of filtering my own words. My eyes met Zarik's for a moment, and I found myself relishing his presence.

I had been completely adrift in the world, but he had looked after me. He had kept me safe, and even comforted me when I simply couldn't take it anymore. But he was so much more than just my protector...there was something about him that was almost magnetic, the pull of his character and body enough to shut down all rationality inside me.

"I didn't do anything," he started to say, but I was no longer listening to him. My eyes were fascinated by his lips and the way they moved, and a second later I was leaning into him, my eyelids drooping as my mouth demanded his.

I stopped when our noses brushed against each other, our lips so dangerously close that I couldn't stop my head from spinning. I had grown accustomed to feeling dizzy and disoriented, but this was completely different...this time it was worth it to have my head spinning.

Neither of us dared to make the first move, to bridge the gap between our mouths, but in the end, we both surrendered at the same time. Our lips touched with a kind of gentleness I didn't expect from Zarik, but I lit a fire under that gentleness of his and fanned the flames.

Parting his lips with the tip of my tongue, l ran one hand down his chest as our kiss became a frenzied one. Our tongues danced eagerly, and my heart kept the tempo as his hands roamed down the sides of my body.

I hadn't expected to feel this comfortable around someone like Zarik but, now that we had kissed, I finally realized it wasn't simply a matter of comfort. Zarik made me feel stronger. He made me believe I could survive whatever challenges life decided to throw my way.

"Thank you, Zarik," I breathed out, slowly breaking away from him.

"What for?" he whispered.

"For being here when I needed you the most..." I paused for a moment and, averting my gaze, continued. "And I'm sorry for this. I shouldn't have—"

"No," he hushed me, laying one finger across my lips. "I won't let you apologize for this, Miri. I had a taste of you, and that's not something I regret. In fact, it's just the opposite."

Pulling me tight against him, my head resting against his chest, he wrapped his arms around me. I felt safe in his embrace, more than I had ever felt since I woke up in those woods, not even knowing who I was. I curled up against him, wishing for that moment to never end, and hummed softly as I felt him caress the small of my back, his fingertips gently brushing against my skin.

"Last night," Zarik said after a few minutes, "you were saying that you remembered. And you seemed scared. I don't know if you want to talk about it, but I'm worried. What exactly did you remember, Miri?"

I hesitated before speaking.

I had remembered a lot, yes, but the memories were more painful than I had expected. I finally had a sense of who I was, where I lived, but the memories of the past few weeks...I didn't remember all of those, but I knew that they were dark. Deep down, I wondered if I didn't remember them because I didn't want to.

"I remember my apartment," I finally said, keeping

my eyes closed as I mentally walked around the place where I had once lived. "I lived alone. And I was alone when..." I trailed off, my heart hammering against my ribs.

"What happened, Miri?"

"I was alone, and then I wasn't," I breathed out. "There was someone else in there with me, but I don't remember who...or even what happened. There's a gap there. But I remember waking up in a cold bed, my wrists tied to the frame."

I gritted my teeth, the panic I had felt then surging once more. The memory of waking up in that bed was a vivid one, and I could still feel the way my wrists had been restrained.

I looked down at my hands by instinct, almost expecting to see my skin chafed from pulling against my restraints. There were a few marks on my wrists, yes, but they were barely noticeable now.

"You don't know who did that to you?"

"I don't," I said as I shook my head. "I remember voices, silhouettes...but I don't remember faces or names."

"What about other details? There might be something in your memories that'll help us figure out where that happened, and where you were before."

"I... I don't remember much," I said. "My memory is spotty. There were more beds around me, and they seemed like the kind of beds you'd see in a hospital. Stretcher beds, maybe. There was the smell of disinfectant, and I remember a plain floor."

"A hospital, then?"

"I don't think so." Pinching the bridge of my nose, I kept my eyes shut as I forced my mind into the past.

"Good, that's good," Zarik whispered, holding me close. His voice was soothing and it made me relax. I took a few deep breaths and more memories started bubbling up to the surface. "What else, Miri?"

"I remember someone holding my arm," I continued. "They checked my pulse, and then they wrapped something around my arm. Like a tourniquet. Then..." I held my breath then, remembering how a needle had punctured my skin. "They injected me with something. I felt nauseous, I felt sick, and I was so afraid..."

"It's okay," Zarik said. "I'm right here. You don't have to be afraid anymore."

"I don't know how long I remained there," I said, the words now flying out from between my lips. "Maybe days. Weeks. I don't know. But I do remember loosening my restraints over time. And one night, I broke free...I dashed out of the room I was in, down a deserted hallway, and then out into the woods. And then...then I just started running."

"Were there more people with you?"

"I... I think so," I nodded.

"Thank you, Miri," Zarik smiled kindly. With his eyes on mine, he leaned down and kissed my forehead. "I know that was hard for you, but I'm glad you shared it with me. We don't have to do it now, and we can wait till you feel ready, but you'll have to share this with the general."

"I will," I replied. "I need to know what happened. I need to know what they did to me."

"We will figure it out, Miri," he said. "And whoever's behind all this...we're going to get them. That's a promise."

ZARIK

I paced back and forth in front of General Rouhr's closed door. Patience had never been one of my virtues.

In fact, I couldn't say I'd ever met a Skotan with a gift for patience.

I didn't want Miri going in there alone. She needed some measure of security. She needed a hand to hold. I paused to wonder if I was underestimating her. In the short time I'd known her, she'd proven that she was brave and resilient. I should start giving her more credit. But I also had this undeniable need to protect her from anything and everything.

When General Rouhr's door opened, I turned around so fast I nearly took out a Valorni coming down the corridor. He gave me a sharp glare but I ignored him.

I was glad to see that Miri wasn't crying, but she did look awfully pale. When she saw me, she immediately came to my side. She gripped my arm, touching her forehead to my shoulder.

"Are you okay?" I asked in a soft voice. She nodded silently. I planted a kiss on the top of her head. I felt her body relax against mine. She felt comfortable with me. Safe. It felt good to be her safe haven. I fought the urge to give her a full kiss. General Rouhr was one of the few people whose opinion I actually cared about. I still needed to have some degree of professionalism.

Miri lifted her chin to look up at me. The sweet look in her eyes was almost my undoing. I couldn't resist pushing a lock of hair back from her face. Professionalism be damned.

"Do I need to leave you two alone for a moment?" General Rouhr asked, one brow arched.

"No, sir," I replied, though I kept Miri close to me.

"Based on the information I've gleaned, I believe that there is a group of humans somewhere purposefully attacking exposed vines of the Puppet Master with hopes of getting it to secrete gas," he said.

"Recreationally?" I asked.

"That could be a component," Rouhr said. "But I

think they are attempting to make a modified version of the memory-erasing gas."

"I doubt they have good intentions," I muttered.

"I agree," he nodded.

"I'm at your disposal if you have a mission for me," I said.

"So am I," came Miri's soft voice. I smiled down at her.

"That's what I was hoping to hear," the general grinned. "Miri, are you up for returning to your apartment? You gave me enough information for me to find it. It's in the southwest section of Nyheim. If that's where you were taken from, your kidnapper might've left something behind."

Miri paused for a moment and sucked in a deep breath.

"I can do that," she nodded.

"If you change your mind at any point, that's perfectly all right." I looked at the general for confirmation. He nodded.

"We'll go as soon as you're ready," I told Miri. She looked nervous, but she managed to smile.

"Wait a moment." General Rouhr stopped us just before we walked away. He held his comm unit in his hand, the notification light blinking.

"Is something wrong, sir?" I asked.

"There was a woman who came in a few days ago looking for her missing daughter. When Miri regained her memory, I reached out to the woman and invited her to come in," he explained. "The timeframe fits."

Of course. Wrapped up in Miri's mystery, I'd forgotten about the woman who started my quest.

"You think she could be my mother?" Miri asked hopefully.

"There's a possibility," General Rouhr said cautiously. "It was more likely when you weren't sure of your name. But it's still worth checking, right?"

Miri bit her lip, thinking. "I'll go see her," she agreed.

"She's in the lobby," the general directed.

Miri and I walked hand in hand to the elevator. A few of the other crew members had gotten used to the sight of Miri and me touching in some way over the last few days, though I still enjoyed seeing the occasional surprised stare.

I never claimed to be a nice person.

The elevator took us down to the lobby. There were often several humans milling about, but the woman General Rouhr had called in would have been easy to spot, even if I hadn't met her earlier.

Her face was drawn and pale. Deep circles showed under watery blue eyes. Her short hair was messy and her clothes were rumpled. She looked like she hadn't had a moment's peace in days.

Her gaze shot toward us when we stepped out of the elevator. I didn't see a gleam of recognition in her eyes. I knew then and there that she wasn't Miri's mother.

"I don't know her," Miri whispered to me, confirming my suspicions.

"What would you like to do?" I asked her. "We can go right back upstairs and get ready to go to your apartment, if that's what you want."

"I can't just leave her there," Miri sighed. "She looks so sad."

"She does."

"I want to go talk to her," Miri decided.

We walked over to the woman together, but I hung back a few feet.

"Hello," Miri said quietly. The woman looked uneasy, like she would fall apart at any moment.

"I know I'm not the person you want to see," Miri continued. "But maybe we can talk. It might make you feel better."

"The only thing that will make me feel better is seeing my daughter again," the woman said in a wobbly voice. There was no anger or malice in her voice. Just sadness and suffering.

"I know." Miri took the seat beside the woman. "I'm sorry I'm not her."

"That's not your fault," the woman cracked a shaky half-smile.

"I know, but I'm sorry all the same," Miri replied.

"I'm sorry I'm not the person you're looking for, either," the woman said. Miri let out a short, dry laugh.

"What's your name?" the woman asked.

"Miri. What's yours?"

"Hileen," she replied.

"Nice to meet you." Miri stuck out her hand for Hileen to shake.

"I wish it were under different circumstances," Hileen replied.

"So do I," Miri agreed.

"They said you lost your memory," Hileen said. "Is that true?"

"It was. Things are coming back to me now, though," Miri replied.

"I hate to ask this of you, but do you remember seeing my daughter anywhere?" Hileen asked. "You were taken around the same time she disappeared. That can't be a coincidence."

"Wherever I was taken, I couldn't see much," Miri said. "I think there were other people with me, but I was blindfolded and restrained most of the time."

"Oh god," Hileen sobbed.

"I'm sorry!" Miri gasped. "I shouldn't have said that. I'm so sorry." She immediately put her arms around Hileen. I expected her to push Miri away, but instead, Hileen leaned in. She cried into Miri's neck. Miri rubbed her back and murmured soothing consolations.

"It's the not knowing that's the worst part," Hileen sobbed. "I can't sleep. I can't be away from my comm unit for even a moment out of fear that she might try to reach me."

"I know," Miri nodded.

I watched Miri and Hileen in stunned silence. It amazed me that Miri was able to comfort a stranger with no hesitation. I'd seen my fair share of distressed family members during my career, but I never knew what to say to them when I delivered bad news.

Miri had been through hell and she still had a good, gentle heart. That was a rarity.

Guilt gripped me once more. My feelings for Miri had grown considerably over the last few days.

I could say with complete honesty that I was no longer in this to regain my honor. At this point, I rarely thought about it. It mattered more to me that Miri was taken care of.

I reflected on who I used to be and shuddered in disgust. I was so selfish and self-pitying. I never expected my bitterness to fade away into anything else, let alone happiness.

That first kiss with Miri was the happiest moment of my life. I wanted to live in that happiness forever, but I shouldn't be allowed to have it. I didn't deserve it after all of the mistakes I've made. Mistakes that cost others their lives.

The happiness Miri had given me was a priceless treasure and I'd stolen it away like a thief in the night.

And I had no plans to ever let it go.

MIRI

"Is this the place?" Zarik asked me, pointing with his chin toward the door to the center of the triplex in front of us. Grayish and bland, like most of southwest Nyheim, it was exactly as I remembered it to be.

That was a first.

I eyed the number next to the door, as if to confirm this was my house, and then laid one hand on the handle and turned it.

The door didn't budge. It was locked.

And I had no idea where the key was.

"I can take care of that." Gently pushing me out of the way, Zarik's eyes homed in on the spot where the lock would be. I saw him tense up, probably readying himself to kick the door open, but I placed one hand on his shoulder and stopped him.

"We don't need to do that," I said, going down on one knee. The motion felt familiar, and I let my unconscious mind guide my hands as I plucked a loose tile off the wall. Hidden behind it was a flat metallic key, one I knew would open my apartment's door.

"A spare, huh?" Zari said, nodding approvingly. "Your memories...they're still coming."

"They are," I smiled. "There are some things I still don't remember, but it's all coming back. I can feel it." Turning the key in my fingers, I held my breath as I slid it into the lock. Turning it, I pushed the door open and it swung back easily on its hinges. "And here we are. Home sweet home."

It felt weird to be back in my place. The smell was familiar—lavendrew and pinor—and the furniture was exactly where I remembered it to be. The old two-seat sofa pushed against the wall, its springs squeaky and tired; the small wooden table beside the kitchen counter, unread books strewn across its surface; an abandoned laundry basket in the corner.

I kicked my shoes off as I stepped inside, the cold tiles underneath my feet somehow grounding me to reality. I made my way into my bedroom and pushed the door open with the tip of my foot, somehow hoping that whatever I'd found there would give me some answers. But no: my bed was made, and the room was as tidy as I had left it. There was no information to be gained there.

"See anything?" Zarik asked me from the adjoining kitchenette. Pursing my lips, I just shook my head. We'd thought coming here would help—maybe my kidnappers would've left something behind—but it seemed like this was a fool's errand.

Dragging my feet back to Zarik, I let out a sigh and threw myself on the sofa. Cautiously, Zarik sat beside me. He turned around to face me and rested one hand on my knee, his eyes on mine. "Are you okay?" he asked me. "It must be odd for you to be back here."

"A bit," I admitted.

The apartment was mine—my memories told me so —but it also seemed like it belonged to some other Miri.

It was an odd feeling, but I couldn't stop myself from drawing a line between the Miri from a few weeks ago and the amnesiac woman I had become. They were one and the same, yes, but I was having a hard time adjusting to that reality.

"Do you see anything that might be out of place?" Zarik continued. He was trying hard not to sound inconsiderate, but I knew he was aching for some answers.

And, God, so was I.

I looked around once more, but nothing grabbed my attention. Everything seemed tidy—I had been cleaning the apartment the day I 'disappeared'—and everything was in its rightful place. I even looked at the floor, hoping to see some dirty footprint or a lock of hair that wasn't my own, but there was nothing.

"It's useless," I groaned. "We're not going to find anything here."

"But we will," Zarik said, sounding more confident than I expected him to be. "Let's just try and think about what might've happened. Are you sure someone broke in?"

"I don't remember exactly, but that must've been it," I replied.

"There's just a slight problem with that theory," Zarik whispered, more to himself than to me. Slowly getting to his feet, he walked toward the door and examined it for a couple of seconds. "It doesn't look like someone broke in. The doorframe, the lock, even the latch, are all in perfect condition."

"Maybe they used lockpicks?"

"I don't think so." Going down on one knee, he eyed the lock directly. "If they had, there would be some marks. But there's absolutely nothing in here. Maybe someone knew about your spare key?"

"Impossible. I'm super careful about that."

"Then..." He trailed off, the gears inside his head

turning as he tried to come up with another scenario. "Does anyone else have a key? A friend, or maybe a family member?"

"Yes," I frowned, not liking what Zarik's question seemed to hint at. Could someone from my personal life be behind my kidnapping? "My cousin, Kyle, has another key, just in case something happened to me."

"And you're close, the two of you?"

"Yes," I said. "So there's no way he was behind this. It's just impossible."

"We have to consider every possibility, Miri. I know it's not pleasant to think that—"

"I get it," I cut him short. "I just don't like it. Do you have your comm with you? I'll just give my cousin a call and we'll put this to bed."

"Okay," he nodded, grabbing his comm from his pocket. "He might not tell you the truth, though."

"If he's lying, I'll know," I said, grabbing the comm from his hands and inputting my cousin's contact information from memory. It seemed that I was getting better and better with each minute that passed. The only memories that seemed almost impossible to grasp were the ones following my disappearance...and I suspected that was because those events had happened shortly before I was injected with the memory-loss toxin.

"Miri?" A female voice burst from the comm. Not

my cousin's voice, that was for sure. "I've been trying to reach you for ages! Is everything alright?"

"Yes, aunt," I said, not wanting to explain the whole story over the comm. "I just had to go away for a couple of days. Is Kyle around? I need to speak with him."

"That's why I've been trying to reach you, Miri!" she cried out, a sense of dread to her words. "I haven't heard from him for days now! He said he was heading over to spend time with that friend of his, Dreve, but I'm not sure I've ever really liked that boy. But that was days ago!"

My heart rate shot up the moment I heard her words.

Kyle was missing?

Whatever happened to me, did it get him, too?

Oh no.

Did I leave him behind?

Or was it just a coincidence?

"I... I'll try to see what I can find," I interrupted her, and she seemed to calm down at that. I promised I'd let her know the moment I had some information, and then handed the comm back to Zarik.

I stood in the middle of my living room, completely frozen. I was trying to process everything, but my brain circuitry was starting to break down.

Why had my cousin disappeared, too?

What was the meaning behind all this?

Oh, God, what a mess.

"I can't stand this," I whispered, one lone tear already rolling down my cheek. "This is too much."

ZARIK

Miri stood in the center of her living space looking small and sad.

And unbelievably beautiful.

I closed the distance between us in a single stride and wrapped her in my arms. She leaned into me. I felt her chest expand as she took slow, deep breaths.

"It's okay to cry if you need to," I told her.

"I'm tired of crying. I feel like I've been crying for days," she said. "I can't believe I have any tears left at all."

I disliked the sound of human crying, but it was especially unpleasant when Miri cried. It wasn't unbearable because the sound annoyed me. It was unbearable because when she cried, the light left her eyes.

"That's okay, too," I told her. We fell silent for a long while. I wasn't sure what to say. I knew how to comfort her when she was in distress or frightened, but I'd never seen her like this before. She was like a shell of herself.

"What should I do?" I asked her.

"What you're doing is exactly what I need," she replied. Her cheek felt warm against my chest, even through the tactical shirt I wore. It was nice to feel some warmth in her. She'd spent too long feeling cold.

As I held her, I wondered if I'd underestimated humans as a whole or if Miri was simply extraordinary.

From the moment she woke up in the forest with no memory until right now, she'd experienced more shock that most humans experienced in their lives.

I'd learned that shock affected every aspect of a human, especially the mind. Shock from traumatic experiences had driven humans mad before. I could tell the weight of it all had taken its toll on Miri, but she was far from giving up.

A flicker of guilt distracted me from my thoughts of her.

She still believed I had taken an interest in her case out of selfless kindness.

Her mental image of me was a dishonest one. That wasn't fair to her.

I wasn't sure what she'd been through exactly, but it was something horrible. A betrayal.

For that alone, she deserved to know the truth. She didn't deserve to have anything even remotely horrible happen to her ever again.

Miri let out a soft sigh, pulling me from my thoughts. I automatically looked down at her, ready to assess her needs. I found her looking up at me. Her lips weren't pulled up at the corners, but I still felt her smile. Her eyes were warm and filled with trust.

Once again, I was reminded of how good it felt to protect someone and not screw it up. For the first time in years, I felt like I was worth something to someone.

I'd never be able to repay Miri for giving that back to me.

I slid my hand up her back and over her shoulder so I could gently stroke her cheek. Miri tipped her head slightly in the direction of my hand and let her eyes flutter closed. She looked more relaxed than I'd ever seen her.

Her eyes opened slowly. I gazed at her stunning face a moment longer before lowering my lips to hers.

The moment our lips touched, it was as if everything was made right with the world. My honor, her amnesia…those became nothing but small details. She gently laid one hand on my chest, and I knew she was feeling my heart beating under her fingertips. It was a simple gesture, but one that made me want her even more than before.

"Zarik," she whispered against my lips, the sound of her voice enough to make me forget about the world around us.

I had never understood why hardened soldiers like General Rouhr or Sylor had fallen for such fragile creatures as human females were...but now I saw it all so clearly.

Miri was perfect in her frailty, and the more her world seemed to collapse around her, the more I wanted to protect her.

She didn't need it; her strength was part of her beauty.

But I'd never want to stop trying.

"I'm right here," I whispered back at her, enjoying the way I had my arms wrapped around her delicate body. It felt right to hold her, to have her body against mine, and I found myself wanting more. I wanted my naked skin on hers, to run my fingers through her hair, and to hold her while I kissed her.

I wanted to make her mine.

There was something about her that awoke my most primal urges, and I knew that the more I stayed close to her, the more the need to make her my mate would tear at me.

It wasn't fair to her...and yet, I couldn't stand the thought of being away from her.

"I will make it right," I promised her, holding her face with both hands as I looked into her eyes. "I don't care what it takes, Miri, but I will make it right."

"I know you will." Laying her head against my chest, she closed her eyes and took a deep breath. Her chest rose and fell at a steady pace, the warmth of her body seeping into mine, and I had to use all of my willpower to restrain myself.

I was on the verge of pushing her back against the wall, my fingers twitching as I yearned to rip the clothes off her body. I wanted to see every curve of her naked body, I wanted to taste every inch of her, and I wanted to make her moan and scream.

And she wanted answers.

Whatever she wished.

"We should get going," I forced myself to say. As much as my body craved her, I knew I had to keep my head on her problems. Miri needed me to think rationally, and I wasn't about to let her down. She had no memories, she didn't know if she could trust her family or friends, and the only person she could rely on was me.

Honor. That used to be the thing I prized the most in the whole world. But now things had changed.

Honor was nothing but a fleeting concern...because

what I really wanted now was to put a smile on her face.

And nothing would stop me from doing it.

Absolutely nothing.

By the time we left the apartment, I was feeling much better.

Zarik's kisses were therapeutic, no doubt about it. And I was in dire need of that kind of therapy.

Still, duty called.

We didn't have a lead on my cousin, so we decided that our best course of action would be to investigate the surroundings of the small outpost I was found in.

Zarik was distracted with his comm for a while, asking headquarters for a rift to be opened, and we waited as the request was relayed to someone called Fen.

A few seconds later, light was emanating from a thin line in front of us, like a crack in space. It widened by a few feet, showing the main street of the settlement on the other side, and I held my breath as we walked into it.

I didn't like it, but I was starting to grow accustomed to travelling by rift.

It was convenient and faster than anything I could imagine.

Still, that cold feeling was annoying: even though the sun was burning brightly, I couldn't help but shiver. I wrapped my arms around myself and let out an "I'm fine" before Zarik could even open his mouth.

"Good," he nodded. "That's the herbalist's store, right?"

"It is," I replied, already looking at the small entrance to Kanna's herbal shop. A small sign with her name hung over the door, and the curtains behind the bay windows were drawn back to reveal an assortment of jars on display.

So many details I hadn't noticed before, when my mind was in a blank panic.

I could see her moving behind the counter, rearranging items on the shelves.

"Let's go, then," Zarik said, leading the way. He climbed the short set of stairs leading up to the shop and I trailed after him. Kanna spun around when the bell above the door chimed, but she frowned when she saw Zarik.

"Please tell me you're here as a paying customer,"

she sighed. When I stepped out from behind Zarik, her eyes landed on me and her frown transformed into a smile. "Miri! You look good! I take it our friend here is treating you well."

"He is," I smiled.

"I can see that. You look so much better. Your memories?"

"They're returning," I said. "Slowly, but steadily."

"Good. Why are you here, then? Something I can help you with?"

"Hopefully," Zarik replied in that curt manner of his. "Did you notice anything suspicious when Miri came into town?"

"Well, I did see an amnesiac girl run out from the woods," she chuckled, her arched eyebrows a worthy addition to her amused grin. "Aside from that, nothing else."

"Can you describe what happened?"

"I was minding my own business," she started, "when I saw her barrel out of the woods. I was pushing my cart back into the store and I stopped to see what was happening. The guards pointed at Miri, she got scared, and then she ran straight past the guards and knocked down my cart. The rest you already know: the guards contacted you, and you came."

"Thank you, Kanna. That helps," I told her, even though it was a lie.

She hadn't seen anything that I didn't remember, and so we remained completely clueless. Still, she had been kind to me and I felt like I had to be kind to her as well. "If there's anything else, anything at all, just let me know."

"Well, I've noticed a few strangers around these parts lately," she muttered, looking up at the ceiling as if trying to recall whatever it was. "New faces. Young men, mostly."

That was enough to grab my attention.

"What can you tell me about them?"

"Not much, really," she shrugged. "They just come into town from time to time, looking scruffy as hell. They buy a few supplies, and then they head out fast. They don't linger, you see. In a settlement like this, whoever wanders in usually stays for a night or two before heading out again. These guys, they always seem to be in a hurry."

"And do you have any idea where they might have come from? Or where they go after leaving here?"

"I know a group of them came into town a few days ago, and they bought all the food they could carry. They looked antsy, and they spent a lot of time looking around, almost as if they expected to find someone. Anyway, they were also looking for some tech replacement parts, but we don't have a lot of that around here. As far as I know, they headed to the nearest settlement, a day's journey from here. There's a junkyard there."

"Another settlement?" Zarik frowned as he stood next to me. He checked something on his datapad quickly, the creases in his brow deepening, and then returned his gaze to Kanna. "I don't find any sign of a second settlement on the map."

"But it's there," she replied. "It's a new settlement, so maybe that's why your map doesn't show it. Some people started scavenging for old parts after the war, and there was a lot of old tech lying around where the settlement is. One thing led to another, and now you have a small town there."

"Do you know how to get there?" I asked her. This could be the lead we were looking for.

"Of course, dear," she smiled kindly. "It's mostly rough men there, but even they need the care of a good herbalist from time to time. Made some money from them, that I have." Turning her back to us, she grabbed a piece of paper from under her counter and started scribbling something on it.

One quick glance at Zarik was enough for me to notice his frown. He didn't like Kanna's crude map, as he was used to military precision, but it wasn't like we had a choice. "There you go. It's about a day on foot, so you should be on your way if you still want to make it before night. The forest is quieter now, less trouble than we used to have with the sorvuc. But I'd still be careful after dark."

"Thank you," Zarik and I said in unison. Grabbing Kanna's map from the counter, Zarik looked at it for a couple of seconds and then smiled at the old woman before marching out of her store. I followed after him, using my hand to shield my eyes from the sun.

"We could be onto something."

"Right," he grunted, once more looking at the map in his hands. "Too bad we'll have to go the long way."

"Why? Can't Fen's program open a rift?"

"Not without precise coordinates, it can't." With a deep sigh, he straightened his back and let his gaze roam to the settlement's gate. "So we'll have to walk."

"Then we walk." Smiling, I closed the distance between us and grabbed his arm. I looked up into his eyes until he finally returned my smile, his expression easing, and we walked out of the settlement side by side.

As much as I wanted to find out what the hell had happened, I was actually feeling happy Zarik and I would get to spend a full day together.

He was the only anchor I had in this world, and I was growing to like his presence more and more.

ZARIK

I t was hard to believe, but I was actually pleased we couldn't use the rift to travel.

I knew Miri was desperate for answers, but I couldn't help but fear that those answers would tear us apart.

After all, who knew what secrets her past held? It was hard to tell what would happen once we dragged the truth into the light and, just for the time being, I was happy to spend time with her without having to worry about that.

Our trek took us onto a narrow path that snaked through the forest, taking us over low hills and wide clearings, the vegetation around us lush and vibrant. It was hard to believe that just a few months ago the Xathi roamed this place, bringing chaos and destruction in their wake. For a moment, I understood the rage and impotence some of the anti-alien groups felt toward us.

Even though we had done it unwittingly, there was no arguing the fact that the Xathi had only landed on this planet because of us. But it wasn't like we'd had any choice.

We saw a chance to strike back at them, a chance to end a war that had cost the Allied worlds more than we could endure, and we took it.

Wouldn't the humans have done the same, were they in our shoes?

"What are you thinking about?" Miri asked me as she ducked under a low hanging branch, the orange glow of a setting sun already coloring the whole forest. A few leaves fell on her hair as she rose and, with a chuckle, I brushed them off her, enjoying the way my fingers felt against her skin. I just wanted to grab her, to take hold of her and let my urges take over.

And every time we exchanged a glance, I couldn't help but think that she wanted the same.

But I couldn't do anything.

I *wouldn't* do anything without first solving the riddle that her life had become.

"I was thinking that it's hard to believe the Xathi were ever here," I finally answered her, grabbing her hand to help her over a fallen tree trunk. Once more, I felt electricity crackle under my skin as she nestled her fingers in the palm of my hand, and I had to take a deep breath to control myself. "Your planet is beautiful, Miri. Too bad no one seems to have the time to enjoy it anymore."

"That's true," she whispered softly, her eyes focused on the path ahead of us. For a few minutes, she said nothing. "Do you ever regret coming here?"

"What do you mean?"

"It's not like you can go back, right?" she asked, her eyes burning with curiosity. "Evie says you're all trapped here. Even if you wanted to go back home, it's not like you'd be able to."

"That's true. But I try not to think of it," I replied with a shrug. "How do you humans say it? No use in crying over spilled milk, right? Besides, I like your planet. And I have the guys with me."

"The guys, huh? It doesn't feel like you're that close to them."

"It's...complicated." I paused for a moment, trying to think of what to say. Could I really tell her that I was a man without honor? That my presence was of no consequence to the teams? Would she think less of me if she knew? "I just like to do my own thing."

"Which is?"

I was about to reply when we finally heard something other than small wild animals. I froze in my tracks, and Miri bumped against me from behind.

Holding one hand up in the air, I ensured she didn't say a word as I tried to listen to that sound, whatever it was. It was metallic and rhythmic, almost like someone was banging against a metal plate.

Kanna had said the settlement owed to its origins to scrappers, so the sound had to mean we were close. According to her terribly drawn map, we were somewhere in the settlement's vicinity.

"Let's continue," I told Miri. "But quietly now." She did as I told her, and I breathed out in relief at that. As much as I enjoyed talking with her all day, her questions about my past were leaving me on edge.

I didn't want to lie to her, but I didn't want to tell her about the real Zarik.

After a few more minutes of walking, the narrow path we were on finally gave way to another clearing. This one, though, was unlike the others we had passed through.

Instead of a carpet of grass and fallen leaves, metallic scrap littered the ground as far as the eye could see. Old machinery and broken parts had been piled as high as some trees, and some of those piles were part of some improvised settlement walls.

Working in front of those walls was a burly man. He wasn't wearing a shirt, and there was a heavy sledgehammer in his hands. Moving fast for a man his size, he repeatedly smashed the sledgehammer against a large metallic panel, trying to shape it into something else.

Only when he noticed me staring did he stop swinging the hammer.

I tensed under his gaze, not knowing how to react. As far as I knew, this settlement could be some kind of haven for anti-alien activists.

"Oy!" The man cried out, wiping the sweat off his brow with the back of his hand. Grinning wildly, he gestured for Miri and me to walk toward him. "Don't be afraid. I'm a big fellow, but you're even bigger!"

Relaxing, I exhaled with relief and started walking toward the man, careful not to bump against any of the old machinery strewn across the ground.

"Sorry to disturb you," I started, only to find my hand in the man's grip. He shook it heartily, slapping my arm repeatedly as he did it.

"No need apologizing, friend," he interrupted me. "Not many people come through these parts, so it's always a pleasure to see a new face. Or new faces, I should say," he continued, now turning his attention to Miri. Letting go of my hand, he gave her a polite bow and a smile. "The name's Arken, and I'm in charge of this settlement. If you can call it a settlement, that is. Are you looking to buy or to sell?"

"Neither," I replied, and disappointment washed across the man's face. Clearly, he'd hoped that we were customers. "We just came here to ask a few questions, if that's okay. Kanna told us that—"

"Kanna, that old hag!" he laughed. "How is she? I haven't seen her for a while. I hope my last workers didn't scare her off. Bunch of assholes, the lot of 'em. Got nicer folk now, thankfully."

"She's, huh, fine."

"We're looking for some men that might have come here, looking to buy some parts just a few days ago," Miri jumped in. The man was clearly a talker, and I was glad that Miri had decided to take the reins of the conversation. "Scruffy-looking men. Young."

"Ah, yes, yes," Arken replied, running one hand through his already disheveled hair. "Bunch of assholes, too. It seems like a junkyard is an asshole-magnet. I should've opened a bakery, you know? I'd be dealing with much nicer fellows, and the work wouldn't be as heavy."

"About these men," I said, clearing my throat as I interrupted him. "What can you tell us about them? We would really like to find them."

"I can tell you a few things about them," he nodded. "But night's falling, and you'd be foolish to go anywhere at this time. So come with me, and I'll have the missus serve you dinner and prepare you a place to spend the night."

"Thank you but—"

"Lovely," Miri said, cutting me short. "We really appreciate it."

Sighing, I watched as Miri followed Arken past the outer walls and into the settlement. I had no choice but to go after her.

MIRI

If it were up to Zarik, we would have gotten our answers and marched right back into the forest. As for me, I wanted the moment to last, even if just for a couple of hours more.

And as I followed Arken into his little settlement, which was nothing but a mess of odd-looking houses he had built with whatever he found from old abandoned shuttles, I was happy I had made that call.

The settlement wasn't really a town—only Arken and his family lived here, aside from a few hired hands —but there was a charm to it.

If you looked past all the junk he had collected over the months, the place had a certain quaintness to it. More than just that, the laughter of Arken's numerous family drifted into the main street, and I immediately knew I was in a place where happiness was the norm.

"Collecting strays again, Arken?" A woman as burly as Arken was greeted us from the door of a two-story house. Her voice was loud and vibrant, but her expression was an open one. She was wearing an apron and had her long hair tied in a bun.

"And they're hungry, too, Misa."

"We don't want to be a lot of trouble," I said meekly, but the woman just waved me down.

"Nonsense," she said. "We love having visitors. Come in, come in."

After some awkward introductions—Zarik wasn't used to such boisterous humans, it seemed—we finally settled around a large dinner table with Arken's family.

There was his wife and his two brothers, and then a mixture of Arken's sons and nephews. There were only a few women in the house, but they were as loud as the men were.

Although Zarik tried to get some answers, Arken refused to do it before dinner. That didn't end up being a problem.

As Misa served us all a delicious stew, Zarik quickly forgot all about the mission and devoted all his attention to devouring whatever was being put on his plate.

Not that I could accuse him of anything, as I was

pretty much doing the same thing. After a whole day trekking through the wilderness, I was hungry as hell.

"Alright, Arken," Zarik spoke up after dinner, one hand draped over his stomach. "Dinner was amazing, but we have to talk about these men that came here."

"Of course, my friend," Arken nodded solemnly. "I figured one day a fellow like you would come looking for them. They're a nasty bunch, that they are."

Zarik sat straight almost immediately, and I did the same.

Whatever Arken knew, it sounded promising.

"What do you mean?" I found myself asking him, my heart already beating fast.

"Don't know much about them, but they asked me a lot of questions about the aliens and whatnot," he explained. "Said a lot of nasty things as well. I don't care for that. As far as I see it, fellows like you," he pointed at Zarik, "are the reason me and my family are alive."

"Thank you," Zarik smiled.

"No need for that. Anyway, they came here looking for a couple of generators and some more spare parts. My sons have found a group squatting in some abandoned buildings a few hours away from here, so I guess those men came from there. They're probably building a settlement of their own."

"Do you know where that is?" With both his elbows

on the table, Zarik was already leaning forward, almost as if he was ready to pounce on Arken's next words.

"Three hours on foot from here, just head northwest on a straight line and you'll find it. Can't go wrong, really."

"Thank you." Pushing his chair back, Zarik rose to his feet and looked at me.

"Whoa, slow your horses," Arken laughed. "You're crazy if you're thinking of heading out tonight. Not even a full moon out there. The forest is quieter than it used to be, but not that quiet."

He shook his head. "If you're trying to get the jump on those fellows, a flashlight will give you away. It's your choice, but if I were you, I'd spend the night."

"That's very kind but…" Zarik trailed off, his lips a tight line as he wrestled with the urge to go out on a hunt. We were so damn close to finding some answers that a whole night of waiting seemed like a nightmare. "We accept your offer, Arken. Thank you."

Roaring his enthusiasm, Arken then dashed toward the kitchen and returned with a bottle of brandy for a celebratory toast. The whole family joined in, as well as Zarik and I, and only then did Misa guide us toward the room where we'd spend the night.

"Not much, but it'll do," she announced kindly as she opened the door to a small bedroom, nothing but a tiny little bed pushed against one of the walls. Too embarrassed to ask for separate beds, Zarik and I simply mumbled our 'thanks'.

When she left, Zarik immediately turned to me, a serious expression on his face.

"I can sleep on the floor. You take the bed."

"Nonsense," I laughed. "We'll both fit in there."

One look at the bed and it was obvious that we wouldn't. Still, Zarik didn't protest. He settled onto the mattress, occupying the whole bed, and I joined him under the blankets, holding him tight so that I wouldn't fall off during the night.

The faint outline of scales over his chest tempted me, so I ran my hand over him sleepily. "Sorry," I mumbled. "That was probably rude."

"Not at all." Zarik's voice sounded tight, tense, but our long walk had done me in.

With my head resting on his bare chest, the sound of his lazy heartbeat as my lullaby, I quickly found myself drifting off to sleep.

Tomorrow would be reckoning day.

But tonight...tonight was just ours.

———

"JUST FOLLOW that direction and you'll be there soon enough," Arken said, pointing into the distance. Just a stone's throw from the walls of the settlement, the vegetation rose again, green and wild and ready to claim what belonged to Mother Nature.

Or to the Puppet Master, really, if what I understood about that situation was correct.

"Thank you so much," I said, my eyes jumping from Arken to his wife. The two had accompanied me and Zarik to the edge of their settlement, and had even given us some food for breakfast.

They had insisted for us to share breakfast with them, but both Zarik and I were too restless to accept their invitation.

We were close to finding some answers, and were aching to do so.

After promising Arken we'd come and visit one day in the future, Zarik and I finally started marching northwest. It didn't take long before he noticed a trail.

"Right there, see it? A few branches are broken, and some of the damage goes as high as your shoulders. That means someone around your size has walked through here. Probably someone from Arken's family, or maybe one of the guys we're chasing after. Either way, I'm willing to bet this trail will lead straight toward the abandoned buildings Arken told us about. All we have to do is follow it."

"Let's do it, then."

"Are you sure you want to come with me?" he asked me, looking at me with a hesitant expression. "You can wait for me in the settlement. I know Arken and his family would be happy to have you, and I can follow this trail by myself and—"

"No," I stopped him. "I want to see where the trail leads. And I want to be there when you find the lab or whatever that place was. I want to see it with my own eyes. Maybe that way I'll remember everything."

More than anything, I needed to know *who* exactly was behind it all.

"Very well." Grabbing his backpack, Zarik opened it and retrieved a small hatchet.

Suddenly I realized it only seemed small because he was holding it with those massive hands of his: the hatchet looked heavy enough for me to know I wouldn't have been capable of wielding it.

Using it to cut a path for us, he set the pace as we marched forward. My mouth grew dry as I felt twigs breaking under my boots, thorny bushes ripping at my shirt as we went, and flashes of my escape from the lab danced behind my eyes. Still, I gritted my teeth and pressed on. I was tired of being weak. I needed to take back control and start facing the situation head on.

"Are you sure you know where we're going?" I found myself asking Zarik after an hour or so. He seemed to know the exact direction we should follow each time he swung his hatchet. As for me, I still couldn't see the supposed marks of the trail.

I knew Arken had told us to head northwest in a straight line, but it was hard to have any sense of direction this deep in the woods.

"I might not look like it," he replied, throwing me a sly grin, "but I'm an expert tracker."

"I don't doubt it," I chuckled, accepting his hand as helped me jump over a pair of broken trees.

Once more, the touch of his fingers felt just right: it was incredible to think that something as simple as that would be enough to have my heart skip a beat...but that was the truth.

Zarik's touch was enough for me to want more.

To want *him*. Especially after last night. God, it had been both the most amazing and maddening thing in the world to sleep next to him. I still had no idea how I had managed to control myself. Despite my exhaustion, I'd just wanted to press myself against him, to kiss him again, breathe in his scent, and to—

Cool it, Miri, I chided myself. *Remember what you're here for.*

Easier said than done, of course. Every time we touched, I felt a pleasant warmth spread across my body and that warmth was enough for me to forget about my problems. God, I was already missing his lips.

"Get down," he whispered all out of a sudden, immediately going down on one knee. I followed him down, my heart hammering away as I tried to follow his gaze. The vegetation was still thick, but just a little way ahead…

"That's…that's it," I muttered, not even blinking as I stared at the small clearing just a hundred feet away from us.

There were a few squat buildings there, but the one that grabbed my attention was the rusting one in the middle. It looked old, almost as if it had been abandoned years ago, but there were people walking in and out of it.

And there was no question at all in my mind.

"That's the place."

"Are you sure?"

"Yes," I breathed out, panic swelling up in me. I fell back on my ass and, using the heels of my boots to push against the ground, I started backing away. I felt thorns and jagged rocks bite at the palms of my hands, but I didn't even care.

All I knew was that I couldn't be in this place. "They…they were holding me there. I escaped from that building right there, in the center."

"Are you sure?"

I just looked at him and nodded.

Now what?

ZARIK

I moved Miri away from the camp.
I told her it was for her own safety, but I found my own grip on my temper surprisingly weak.

They'd hurt her in there.

They should pay.

I walked us far beyond any human range of hearing and then farther still. We were a good half-mile from the camp before we stopped.

"Tell me everything you remember," I told her.

"There isn't much to say," Miri said. "I was blindfolded when I came in, and when I was in the room, as well. There were definitely other people with me in the room, but they rarely spoke. I never saw the injections coming. They never said anything about what was in them."

"Are you absolutely sure?" I pressed. I didn't like to pressure her. I knew her memory wasn't completely intact yet.

"They mentioned they were low on samples at some point," she said after a thoughtful pause. "They talked about the 'damn plant.'"

"That's good," I smiled. "That's useful. If they're out of samples, they might need to get more. That would put them in the way of the Puppet Master."

"Maybe the Puppet Master can do your team's job and handle the bad guys for us," Miri joked. The fact that she was using humor to cope with her nervousness was a good sign. Every few moments, I could see her blink away tears.

I decided playing along was the best thing for her.

"If only," I chuckled. "I may not be close with my teammates, but I don't relish the idea of them in the line of fire when there's a simpler solution."

As much as I wanted to barrel into the camp, weapons out and ready to kill, I knew that wouldn't help Miri.

The last thing I wanted was for her to be in the forest on her own. Even I wasn't so arrogant as to think that I could take on an entire camp of humans without suffering injury. I especially didn't want to put her through that.

"Either way, it's time to end this." I pulled out my comm unit and gave the strike teams the location.

It was understood that this was not an extermination. No humans were to be killed unless it was absolutely necessary.

Personally, after what these people had done to Miri, I wanted them dead.

But the colder part of me wanted their information more.

The strike teams confirmed the location. They were to come through a rift in a few minutes.

"That's taken care of." I tucked the comm unit away.

"Don't you want to be out there with them?" Miri gave me a curious look.

"I do," I said. "It's funny, I've been waiting so long to get back on a squad and get a chance to be in active combat again." My words trailed away.

"So why aren't you doing just that?"

"Because there's one thing that I want to do more." I smiled down at her.

"What?"

"I want to do what's best for you."

Miri's smile went soft as she rose up on her toes to kiss me lightly.

"I want to go back to the camp," she declared.

"Really?" I was surprised.

"If you can't be out there with your team, the least you can do is keep an eye on them and jump in when needed," Miri reasoned. "You've been so selfless for me. Let me do what I can for you."

"I don't want to put you at risk," I told her.

"I'm willing to bet that the camp members will be too distracted fighting your teammates to notice us lurking in the bushes. And we don't need to be visible. I just want to be in hearing range," Miri said.

"If you're sure." I resolved to pull her away from the camp the moment she showed signs of emotional distress.

We moved carefully through the undergrowth. I scanned the area for any alarm sensors or trip wires that might be hidden.

There were none.

Strange for a camp that had a habit of kidnapping people and messing with their memories against their will. Perhaps they assumed no one would ever come out this far.

Clearly, they'd never intended to let their test subjects go if their memory-loss serum didn't work.

On a hunch, I checked my portable holomap. It displayed everything within a ten-mile radius, yet the camp didn't appear on the grid.

"That's strange," I muttered.

"What's strange?" Miri asked.

"This camp really should be considered a proper settlement. It's certainly big enough. But it's on the map as an abandoned settlement - one that was marked as destroyed by the Xathi," I explained.

"That's not surprising, really," Miri replied. "If you were setting up a camp to perform illegal actions, you'd probably refurbish something rather than build it from scratch."

"Well, yes," I admitted. "But it would be hard to build something this size unnoticed."

"I didn't notice much when I was blindfolded and dragged in," Miri commented.

"Perhaps humor isn't the best coping mechanism for you." I commented as I placed a guiding hand on her back.

"Until I figure out a better one, it will have to do," she shrugged.

"You can always talk to me," I reminded her.

"I know," she smiled up at me. "But if I start talking, I'll start crying. If I'm crying, I'll probably give away our location."

"You make a good point," I conceded. "I'll let it go, just this once."

"Thank you." Miri squeezed my hand. We fell into silence as we neared the camp. I let my thoughts wander back to the formation of this camp.

The question that plagued me still was their motive.

Why would a bunch of humans come all the way out here to experiment with memory loss? They collected samples from the Puppet Master itself. They had to know there was a high chance of perishing.

And kidnapping people? They must've known someone would go looking for them.

It seemed like a high risk without a clear payout. I had to find out what was going on. Miri deserved to know why she was put through all of that.

The strike teams had the camp surrounded. No fighting had broken out yet. I believed Karzin was trying to reason with them, though I couldn't be sure.

His voice didn't carry very well. There were some humans positioned closer to where Miri and I concealed ourselves. Their voices carried perfectly well and they had a lot to say.

"We won't let you leave alive, alien scum!" a male voice snarled. The idiot couldn't tell what he was up against.

"We'll turn your skin into the rugs we wipe our feet on," another spat.

I rolled my eyes. At least they were getting creative with their insults now.

Even if they were disturbingly optimistic.

"Oh, shut up," one of the strike team members growled. It sounded like Axtin. Or maybe Rokul.

"You have no right to be here!" another voice called.

This time it was a female. "This is our home and we want it to be alien-free."

My mind ventured back to a human male that caused trouble a short while ago. Roddik, I think his name was. I didn't deal with him directly, of course. I was still in my self-imposed exile in my workroom at that time. I heard about him through radio traffic and general workplace chatter.

He and a group of followers tried to start a human-only settlement. However, they were nothing more than a band of impulsive drunks with violent tendencies. Naturally, the settlement failed. I wondered if this camp had stemmed from Roddik's vision.

I glanced through a gap in the leaves for a better look at the camp. I got the sense that it had been established for quite some time. Roddik and his followers had been under constant surveillance since they were brought back into Nyheim. If they got word to someone else with instructions to pass on their vision, we would've known about it.

Besides, this camp was much more organized. The residents were altogether smarter than Roddik and his followers, though I used the term smarter very loosely. They still believed General Rouhr and the rest of us were in league with the Xathi with the goal of wiping out humanity.

I looked at the band of aliens surrounding the camp.

It was only a matter of time before we got the answers we needed.

That Miri needed.

MIRI

"They're growing restless," Zarik whispered, his eyes focused on the scene in front of us. The fighting had been brief and brutal.

Even though most of the humans had already surrendered, I could see some lurking beside the rusting building; they didn't seem to have any weapons on them—at least none that I could see—but they looked like they wanted to put up a fight.

"Maybe you should go," I said, doing my best not to let any anxiety show in my voice. I didn't want to be left alone, but I didn't want to be coddled, either.

I knew Zarik was aching to join the fray, and I didn't want to be the one standing in his way. "I think some of those assholes are trying to sneak past the soldiers, Zarik."

"You're right," he sighed, frowning as he noticed one of the men in the camp tucking a gun in his belt and covering it with his shirt. "I need to go. Are you sure you'll be fine? I don't want to leave you, but—"

"As long as you come back to me."

"Count on it, then," he smiled, already getting to his feet. He was about to start moving through the undergrowth and toward the settlement's edge when I stopped him, laying one hand on his shoulder.

"I won't let you go without saying goodbye," I said as I stood up, my eyes locked on his. He looked at me, confusion washing over his face, but I didn't even care. I just reached for him and, holding his face with both hands, went on tiptoes to kiss him.

I closed my eyes as I felt his lips on mine, my heart happily fluttering inside my chest. His hands went down the sides of my body and, grabbing me by the waist, he picked me up. My feet left the ground for a few seconds, and I opened my eyes to find them level with his.

Smiling, I wrapped my legs around his torso and kissed him again, pressing my whole body against his. With my breasts pressed against his chest, I felt the contour of his toned pectorals and ached for more...so much more.

The attraction between the two of us was

undeniable, and I was aching to turn whatever spark there was between us into a raging inferno.

"Be careful," I whispered, my forehead against his. "I don't want you to get hurt. I want you to come back to me, okay? Do that and we'll continue this," I promised him, the hunger in his eyes telling me he would make me keep my promise.

Good—that was exactly what I wanted.

"I *will* come back," he said in that soft but decisive manner of his.

Putting me down, he gave me one final nod and turned around, stalking through the undergrowth and toward the camp. He moved furtively, his attention now fully focused on what would soon become a battlefield, and I felt a nervous tingle in my chest.

There was nothing I could do but wait, though. Taking long, deep breaths, I looked around and spotted a tall tree just a few feet behind me. It had sturdy branches, and their disposition made me believe I could climb up and get a vantage point.

Hurrying, I went toward the tree and, groaning and sweating, somehow managed to climb my way up. Perched on a high, sturdy branch, I was sheltered and hidden while still having a good view of the camp.

The strike teams were trying to herd the humans in front of them into a group, but I could see some trying to slip out from the perimeter. To the side of the main building, four humans hid from sight, and they were clutching what looked like rifles.

They looked nervous, but I knew they were prepared to attack all the same. One of them poked his head out of the corner of the building, momentarily glancing at the alien soldiers, and then went down on one knee and took aim.

I felt my heart skip a few beats as I anticipated what would happen, but then I noticed something in the vegetation right behind the building. "STOP!" I heard Zarik bellow, and his hulking shape jumped out of the shadows and ran straight toward the human.

He tackled him right before the man had a chance to fire, but the three accomplices behind him immediately ganged up on Zarik.

They pointed their guns at him but, knowing that they might shoot their accomplice if they fired, they used the butts of their rifles to hit Zarik repeatedly. I saw him punching his attackers in a whirl of motion.

Oh, my.

My kind, gentle giant was a warrior.

Hearing the commotion, some of the other humans decided to try their luck and grapple the guns away from their captors.

Shots were fired, bodies fell to the ground. I watched it all happen in slow motion, horrified at the scene, but my attention quickly returned to Zarik.

Using the man he had tackled as a shield, he pried the rifle from his hands and fired it against his other attackers.

Two of them fell to the ground, clutching their legs, and the remaining one simply threw his gun down and started running toward the woods.

He was almost there when a green Valorni appeared out of nowhere and tackled him to the ground.

It wasn't much of a fight.

Even though the humans from the camp had the numbers, they were no match for the experience of the strike teams. It took the aliens only a few minutes to subdue the humans, and then they lined them up in front of the main building.

Still holding the same man from before, Zarik shoved him toward the others and then wiped the blood off his lips with the back of his hand.

He didn't seem to be hurt.

He seemed to be enjoying every moment of it.

My chest loosened, but my relief didn't last long.

I was scanning the line of prisoners when I realized there was something eerily familiar about one of them. Holding my breath, I narrowed my eyes into slits and then…

I gasped, finally realizing who I was staring at.

I climbed down the tree I was in as fast as I could and started running toward the camp like a woman possessed. I didn't even notice the way the vegetation seemed to reach for my shirt, thorns ripping holes in the fabric. All I cared about was the man in the camp.

A few aliens wheeled around as I jumped into sight and, even though they looked surprised to see me, none of them stopped me. I made a beeline toward the prisoners and, reaching one of the men, I slapped him so hard that pain shot up my arm.

"You're Dreve," I hissed. "I know you. I've seen you with Kyle. Where is he? What the hell are you doing here?"

"You were an easy target," he spat. "I did what I had to do."

"Yeah?" I threw back at him. "And this is what I have to do."

Cocking my arm back, I punched him straight in the face.

ZARIK

I stepped back, giving Miri room. She deserved it, after everything the bastard had put her through.

And when she was done, I might take a swing myself.

"Was it worth it?" Miri screamed. "Look at you now! You'll never taste freedom again, which is exactly what you deserve since you tried to do that to me!"

Dreve looked shocked.

I wasn't sure if he was more afraid of the prospect of a lifetime in prison, or of Miri.

"Do you even care how many people you've hurt?" she went on. "You disgust me."

By the way he quivered and refused to meet her eye, I could tell he wasn't the leader of this operation. He didn't have the mettle.

He didn't even possess the intelligence to disguise the fact that he'd used Kyle's key to get into Miri's apartment. If he'd smashed the doorframe or broken the lock, we would've never suspected him.

I wondered how he ended up in a place like this, but then I realized that I didn't care. He deserved to rot in a cell, surrounded by the aliens he hated for the rest of his life, for what he'd done to Miri. He deserved worse.

"I think we've found the human in charge," Karzin called from the rusty metal structure. A moment later, two other strike team members appeared, holding a man by the arms. I wasn't sure what I'd been expecting, but I wasn't expecting a portly man, with very little hair, two feet shorter than me.

At first, I wondered how such a weak-looking human could've created a place like this. But then he looked my way. There was nothing in his eyes but coldness and madness. The sick smile on his face was almost as unsettling as his eyes.

He lacked what the humans called a soul. I'd never put much stock into souls until I looked into the eyes of someone who didn't possess one. A shudder passed down my spine. It took a great deal to unsettle me. I was usually the one doing the unsettling.

The team members that held him pushed him to his knees at the feet of Karzin. I suspected they wanted to use his hair to force him to look up, but there wasn't enough of it to get a good grip. Karzin kneeled down enough to grab the man's chin and tilt his face upwards.

"I have a lot of questions for you," Karzin smirked.

"Too bad," the man snarled.

"Let's start with something easy. Does the name Roddik mean anything to you?"

I hadn't expected Karzin to ask about that, though it was a good gateway question. Hopefully, it would lead us somewhere useful.

"He was a moron," the man said with a sneer. "I heard about his failed settlement. We intended to bring them into our fold, but we didn't reach them in time. Though I don't consider it a great loss."

"How did you hear about Roddik?" Karzin asked.

The man responded by spitting at him.

"That wasn't polite," Karzin snarled.

"You savage brutes wouldn't know the meaning of polite." The man rolled his eyes.

"And you do? Last I checked, polite, civilized people don't kidnap innocents to perform sick experiments," Karzin snapped.

"Have you never heard of doing something for the sake of the greater good?" the man asked with a cold smile.

"You know nothing about the greater good," Karzin scoffed. "Why were you injecting your captives with memory-erasing toxins?"

The man stared up at Karzin, silent and defiant. My temper flared. I wanted nothing more than to ram his nose into his skull. I clenched and unclenched my fists. I needed to remove myself from the situation before I did something I would regret.

Actually, that was inaccurate. I would never regret anything I did to that soulless creature.

I wasn't too keen on getting in trouble with General Rouhr, though. We needed the psychopath alive until he gave us the information we needed.

I looked toward the half-collapsed metal building. From what I could tell, no one else was inside investigating it. Surely it contained something useful. Perhaps something inside would lead us to the answers the madman refused to give.

Miri had taken a break from yelling at her cousin's friend, but the look on her face told me she wasn't quite done.

"I'm going to look around in there." I pointed to the structure. "What do you want to do?"

"I'd rather stay here." She took an unconscious step backward when she looked at the structure. "But, what if Kyle's in there? I should go…"

But her feet refused to move her.

"I understand," I assured her. "I'll be right back." I pressed a kiss into her forehead before heading toward the structure.

I couldn't believe it was still standing. Much of the key structural support seemed rusted away. Sharp edges stuck out all over the place. How all of the residents weren't covered in infected scrapes and cuts was a mystery to me.

The inside of the structure was essentially abandoned. The floor was covered in dead leaves that had fallen through the gaping holes in the ceiling and walls. There were a few discarded pieces of broken furniture. From what I could tell, they were using it as a storage space.

That didn't make sense. I had to be missing something.

I examined every detail of the structure. It wasn't very large. It certainly wasn't used for much. Something bad clearly had happened to Miri here.

But where?

I was about to give up when my foot caught on a miniscule rise in the floor. I smoothed away the dead leaves, revealing a wooden square with a handle. A trapdoor.

It was locked, but that wasn't an issue. With one good yank, I separated the handle from the wood, leaving a jagged hole behind. I flipped the door up, exposing a ladder that went straight down into blackness. I heard noises below that sounded like they came from something living.

I hurried down the ladder, well aware that I could be walking into a trap. I stretched my shoulders back, relishing the idea of a good fight. It had been way too long, and that group of humans had been nothing but an appetizer.

But when I reached the bottom, there was only blackness.

The noises were louder but, at the same time, they sounded muffled. I felt along the walls for a light switch. After some blind groping, I found a lever. I pushed it in the only direction it would go. Crude exposed bulbs crackled and lit up. One sparked a bit.

I stood in a room larger than the structure above it. The walls were crammed with overflowing mismatched shelves and tables covered in devices I didn't recognize.

A muffled squeal came from farther inside. I hurried in the direction of the sound. There was a small hallway in the back of the room that led into another chamber. This chamber contained five tables with restraints. Four of the tables were occupied. Humans lay there, restrained and blindfolded. One male. Three females. They were all covered in filth. Even from here I could tell they were underweight.

"I'm here to help!" I called to them.

I went to one of the females first. The restraints had left purple bruising around her wrists and ankles. I let her remove her own blindfold. When she saw me, tears filled her eyes.

"It's over," she said in a hoarse whisper. "It's finally over."

I released the male next, and he helped untie the other females.

"I knew those monsters had the wrong idea about you guys," the man said as he shook my hand gingerly.

"Are you able to climb? The only way out is a ladder," I explained.

They all nodded, two of the women leaning on each other for support.

"Go up to the ladder. If you walk up to anyone that isn't human, they will help you," I told them.

The ragged group gave me one more grateful look before heading toward the ladder.

I thoroughly checked any place big enough to conceal a human, just in case there was someone else I couldn't see or hear. There was no one else.

I looked at the fifth table and a sickening feeling came over me. That table belonged to Miri.

I returned to the main chamber to examine its contents. I realized that the devices littering the tables were outdated lab materials. I began tearing through the crammed shelves and opening every drawer.

I skimmed the contents of the first datapad I discovered. It was an outline for an experiment. The goal was to create a memory-erasing substance that wouldn't be affected by the antidote developed in General Rouhr's lab. That antidote wasn't public knowledge. How did these people know about it?

I continued searching for any useful information. By the time I got through everything, I'd located ten datapads. Some of them were very cleverly hidden. I almost missed the last one entirely. I didn't have the time to read them all, but I was certainly going to bring them back to General Rouhr.

I found a ratty old bag discarded on the floor. It would be just fine for transporting the datapads. Hopefully, General Rouhr wouldn't mind a little grime.

After one final sweep of the room, I made my way to the ladder.

It was time to take Miri away from here forever.

MIRI

"Do you want me to take you back to your apartment?" Zarik asked me.

I stood there, in the middle of the government building's lobby, and shifted my weight from one foot to the other.

I wasn't sure if I could go back, not with all the memories of what had happened feeling so vivid inside my head. It was ironic—in a way, I almost wished I could forget all about Kyle's friend and his stupid actions.

And after all the time and effort trying to get my memories back.

Sigh.

"Is something wrong, Miri?"

"I don't want to go back there," I said as I shook my

head. "At least, not right away. That apartment...it doesn't feel right for me to stay there now."

"I see," he muttered, and I could almost see a thousand thoughts parading behind his eyes. Only after a few seconds of silence did Zarik continue.

"Come with me," he smiled gently, grabbing my hand and leading me down the lobby. I followed him through what seemed like a dozen corridors until we finally stopped before a regular door. "It's not much, but..."

Producing a magnetic key from his back pocket, he slid it across the slit in the panel and the latch popped open with a metallic sound. "My bedroom," Zarik announced, pushing the door open with one hand.

We stepped inside the tiny cramped room and Zarik let out a nervous laugh. "I know. It sucks."

"No, it doesn't," I protested. "This is perfect."

"Good. Then I'll let you have it," he nodded. He was about to turn around and leave when I grabbed his hand.

"Where exactly do you think you're going?" I laughed. "I'm not going to steal your bed away. Besides, I made you a promise...remember?"

"How could I forget?" he asked me softly. Now facing me, he closed the distance between us and laid both hands on my waist. A shiver ran up my spine as I felt the touch of his fingers, and the air around us became electric.

"Good," I whispered, my eyes focused on his lips. God, I was already aching to taste them again. Noticing me looking, Zarik raised one hand and brushed his thumb over my lips, parting them. Then, cupping my cheek with his massive hand, he leaned down and kissed me.

"I'll never get tired of kissing you, Miri."

"I'll make you sure you don't," I teased him, enjoying the way he was smiling at me. There was more than just lust there...Zarik genuinely cared for me, and that in a way I had never experienced before.

Still reeling from our kiss, we slid under the covers, my body craving the comfort of his. I rested my head on his chest and closed my eyes, feeling his heartbeat as he gently ran his fingers through my hair. "Are you okay?" He finally broke the silence between us. "These last few days...I know they were hard on you."

"They were," I said quietly. "I'm remembering more and more...and most memories aren't exactly pleasant ones. There's the Xathi invasion, the periods of hunger, and then this thing with the toxin...I'm becoming numb to it all."

"Then maybe it's time we stop focusing on the bad memories," he said, turning on his side to face me.

"Maybe it's time we start creating good ones." He didn't let me say a word.

He just leaned in and crushed his mouth against mine, his tongue parting my lips at once. Our kiss started wild, and it just grew wilder and wilder with each heartbeat.

I kicked the sheets back in a hurry, eager to see and touch all of his body, and I didn't hesitate before sliding the palms of my hands down his bare chest. In seconds, we were wearing nothing but our underwear, and that made things so much easier—allowing my right hand to explore the region below his waist, I let my fingers fall over the hard shape tenting his boxers. I grabbed it fiercely, curling my fingers against it, and started massaging his cock over the fabric of his underwear.

"You're going to be the end of me," he groaned, weaving his fingers into my hair and pulling on it. I gasped as he pulled my head back, his mouth now busy roaming over my neck, and didn't protest as he unclasped my bra.

My skin prickled as the air in the room caressed my hard nipples and, by the time he pushed my thong down my legs, I was so eager to have him that I couldn't think of anything else.

"Not the end," I moaned softly. "The beginning."

"I like that," he whispered, his lips trailing down my neck toward my breasts. Wrapping his lips around my left nipple, he sucked it into his mouth eagerly, his tongue dancing in circles around it. I tightened the grip I had on his cock and started stroking him harder, my hand moving up and down his length at a steady pace; he was massive, but I already knew that...everything about him told me the word 'average' wasn't something I could use to describe him.

"I want you so much," I found myself saying, pushing his underwear down with frenzied movements. His hard cock sprung free then, falling straight into the palm of my right hand, and I let out a soft moan as I felt its warmth against my skin. "I *need* you so damn much, Zarik."

"Then you're in luck," he growled, his right hand rushing straight to between my legs. "I'm right here." Cupping my aching pussy, he laid his thumb across my clit and applied just the right amount of pressure. I chomped on my bottom lip as my whole body came alive, and I shut my eyes as I surrendered to him.

My moaning turned into screaming the moment he parted my inner lips and slid one finger deep inside me, curling it upward like a hook until he found that secret spot hidden inside me. Pressing it with the tip of his finger, he kept on massaging my clit while his tongue danced with my right nipple. My eyes rolled in their orbits as pleasure took me, and it didn't take long before I was arching my back, my whole body tensing up with anticipation.

"I'm going to…"

I trailed off, ecstasy choking off the rest of my sentence. My heart beat furiously, my blood boiled inside my veins. This was everything I had wished for, and then some more…and we were just getting started.

"Make me yours, Zarik," I whispered, rolling to the side and climbing on top of him. Straddling him, I laid both hands on his chest and looked straight into his eyes. "I don't care about anything else right now. I need to know that I'm yours."

"But you already are," he said, laying one hand around the back of my neck, his eyes never leaving mine. "You were mine the moment I first laid eyes on you. But now…I need you to show me what you want."

"And how exactly can I do that?" I purred, one hand trailing down his chest. Holding his cock once more, I pressed its tip right against my entrance. He was so massive that I wasn't even sure if he'd fit inside me…but I had to try.

"I think you know how," he replied, both his hands on my waist as he pushed his hips off the mattress. I moaned as I felt the tip of his massive cock part my wet pussy lips, and then I cried out with pleasure as, inch by thick, veined inch, he slid his whole length deep inside me. For a split second, I thought he'd tear me in half, but then ecstasy replaced all that nervousness.

"It feels so...good," I panted, my brain still trying to process the way his massive cock was buried deep inside me.

"Make it better," he growled, his hand still around my neck. "Ride me as hard as you can, Miri. You want it just as badly as I do."

"More."

Closing my eyes, I did exactly as I was told. I swayed my hips slowly at first, trying to build a rhythm, but I quickly fell into a frenzied pace. I rode him as if my life depended on it, and he thrust upward with all his might, his cock sliding deep into me.

I wasn't even sure if I was moaning or screaming...all I knew was that my throat felt raw. And still, I couldn't stop.

I kept on riding him until beads of sweat started beading on my forehead and, opening my eyes, I kept them locked on his as we surrendered to each other. In that moment, I felt safe...and, more than that, I felt loved.

"You're like silk," Zarik groaned as I started slowing down. He kept the pace, though, and rolled me to the side, then pinned me against the mattress.

Holding me with my wrists above my head, he

started thrusting wildly, his cock sliding in and out of me relentlessly.

"You have no idea how much I wanted to take you," he whispered into my ear, and that...well, that did it for me. "Touch you." Another shattering pulse as he drove into me. "Taste you."

I was only gasping now, helpless. My eyelids drooped, and a tidal wave of pleasure rose on my mind's horizon. Every single muscle in my body tensed up and, the moment I felt his cock throb violently inside me, I let go.

My moans blended with the sound of his deep breaths, and we dove deep into an ocean of pure lust. We came at the same time, our bodies tangled in a mess of sore muscles and sweaty skin, the scent of pure lust hanging in the air.

Finally, lying side by side, his arms wrapped around me, I felt a sliver of happiness inside me. I had walked through the ruins of my own memories, but it had been a worthy journey...and that was because that journey had given me Zarik.

With that thought burning brightly in my mind, I drifted off to sleep.

ZARIK

The rays of sunlight crept through the window, illuminating Miri's sleeping figure beside me. I sat on the edge of the bed, fumbling through the bedside drawer for my datapad. No new messages appeared on its screen or no flashing red light, so I hadn't been called in to work yet.

She stirred beside me, her hands reaching for the sheet to cover her bare shoulders. She was a perfect picture of contentment, enveloped within the warm bed, her soft lips slightly parted, and her hair swept across her face.

Her skin gave off a slight sparkle as the sunlight hit her naked body. She slowly opened her eyes, squinting at me, her hands grasping at the cold and empty bed next to her.

"Come back to bed, Zarik," she moaned.

I looked at the datapad again to recheck if I was needed somewhere else. It didn't seem like it, so I tossed it back into the drawer and resumed my position next to this morning goddess.

She gazed at me with her dark brown eyes.

"Did I wake you?" I asked as I lay on my side to face her.

She slipped her hands under her head as she looked at me and said, "No, I think I was already half-awake when you got up."

I removed a few strands of hair from her gorgeous face and tucked it behind her ear. If I looked really closely, I could make out a sprinkle of freckles across her nose and cheeks. As if she could get any prettier.

"Do you have to go? Are you needed at work?" she asked.

"No, they can last a few hours without me," I grinned back in response.

Miri smiled and snuggled closer to my chest until her head rested where my heart was beating. She pressed her ear against my skin, her one delicate hand settling on my neck and stroking my hair.

"Your heart is beating very fast," she remarked.

"That's because you're here," I said.

She looked up at me, a slight blush covering her

light freckles. I couldn't make myself look away from the sight of her.

With just that one look, Miri had made feel better than I've felt in years.

When I looked at her, I can think of nothing and no one else but her beautiful figure staring right back at me.

Never would I have believed if I were to tell my past self that this human woman, right before me, would change my life forever.

"Are you alright? You seem quiet," she asked.

"I've never been better," I smiled.

She stroked my cheek, her eyes never leaving mine.

"You're amazing, Zarik," she said. "I've never met anyone like you."

"You think too highly of me," I chuckled.

"That's because you deserve it."

Miri pulled herself up and leaned closer to my face. She placed her nose right on top of mine with a sweet smile fixed on her face. I thought right then and there that if Miri thought of me that way, then that is the only recognition I would ever need.

Nothing else will ever matter.

She continued to drown me with her eyes, looking and feeling more relaxed and content than the first time I saw her. The scent of her body mixed with our sweat from our intimate session last night. I breathed her in and relished every second that I got to spend with her.

She kept her hand on my cheek, gently stroking me with her fingers and humming a sweet song. My eyes wandered to her right arm and to the deep scar running up her forearm. I traced it with my fingertips, causing her to flinch.

"I'm sorry. Did it hurt when I touched you?" I asked.

"Not really," she answered. "It just brought unpleasant memories, which, ironically enough, I still don't exactly remember. I just get this negative feeling from it, you know? I try my best to recall everything, but I can't…"

"Don't force yourself, Miri," I caressed her cheek, "everything will come in time."

I leaned down to her and planted a lazy kiss on her mouth. She slipped the tip of her tongue out and gave me a lick on my lower lip before I leaned back. I laughed at her naughtiness and noted her cheeky behavior.

"You know, we can't stay in bed forever," she said.

"I know, but I would love to," I wrapped my arm around her waist and pulled her even closer. "I'd hate to get called for another assignment right now, when I know you'll be here waiting for me."

Her warm body fused with mine and I could just feel the passionate fire smoldering between us.

"Does General Rouhr usually give you multiple cases at the same time?" she looked up and asked.

I nodded and said, "Yeah, oftentimes that's what happens, but other times, when our plate still isn't full, we handpick some cases ourselves."

"Was that what happened with me?"

"What do you mean?" I asked.

"Were you assigned to my case, or did you take it up on your own?" she clarified.

I fell silent for a few seconds before I could answer.

"I took it up on my own," I finally answered.

"Why?" she asked further.

I gulped and felt a ball of stone forming inside my stomach.

I knew this was bound to happen.

We'd come too far, done too much, for me to lie to her.

And not telling her the whole truth was the same as lying.

"Miri, you have to understand," I started, "in order to answer that, there's something you must know."

"What is that?" her eyes looked worried now.

I felt a punch of guilt to the stomach. I hated making her worry.

"My history isn't what you would call spotless," I continued. "Before the Xathi attack, I was assigned a number of independent missions. Mostly protective details."

It had been so long ago. But I could still see the blood.

"The mission was to protect a family. Mother, father, two little girls. The mother was in the diplomatic core."

Miri's fingers laced through mine. I paused to stroke her hand with my thumb while I could still touch her.

"I got a message and left the family. It was a decoy." There were no words, not really. I could make all the excuses in the world, about how it seemed like the right move at the time.

But it all came down to one simple fact.

"I failed. They were all killed."

Her sharp gasp brought me back to the present.

"With the Xathi invasion imminent, the military wasn't eager to get rid of any soldiers. But they stripped me of my honors."

"But what if it wasn't your fault?" she demanded.

"It was," I said. "They trusted me. I was shunned for years. My shame kept me isolated, even when the rest of the crew might have forgiven the past." I inhaled deeply, breathing in her scent.

"When your case came up, I requested it. It was an opportunity to redeem my lost honor."

"W-What?" she choked.

"Miri, please understand," I tried to comfort her. "That's how it started, I won't lie to you. But I swear it was only like that at first. I thought that maybe, if I could solve this case, General Rouhr would give me back –"

"I don't think I want to hear this," she cut me off and rose from the bed.

"Wait, Miri, please listen!" I sat up after her and started looking for my pants. "You have to understand, I didn't know you back then, I thought it was going to be –"

"Oh, so would that have made a difference?" she turned and snapped at me.

Miri's face was flaming red, and tears formed at the edge of her eyes as she scrambled about the room looking for her clothes.

"Miri, please!" I begged. "I was trying to regain my good standing with the general, but then I got to know you and that changed everything! You're more than I thought you'd be!"

"What?" she scoffed at me. "You thought I'd be? Oh, so let's say I didn't meet your expectations, would I have been another case to you?"

"Well, no, it's not like that –"

"God, I feel so used!" she cried out as she pulled the shirt over her head. "And here I thought you were helping me out of the goodness of your heart, only to find out you were just using me as a stepping stone to get your damn honor back!"

"Miri, I'm sorry," I grabbed her arm. "It's not like that. I like you. I -- I want to be with you."

"How can I believe that?" she said, her eyes glaring with accusation. "When you haven't been honest with me all along? I can't believe I've been this stupid, exposing myself to some guy I barely know when I should've been more careful!"

I closed my mouth, unable to find more words to say.

She was right – I should've been honest and clear with her from the start. But how was I supposed to know I was going to end up falling in love with her?

"Miri," I reached out for her again, "please just give me time to explain. Please give me another chance to prove it to you."

"Okay, so answer this one question for me," she said, her hands fixed firmly on her hips. "When were you ever planning on telling me this if I hadn't asked?"

"I-I don't know," I admitted.

"So, were you planning on keeping that secret for the rest of your life?" she scoffed. "Wrong answer, Zarik, very wrong."

"Please, just give me some time to make it up to you –"

"You don't have to," she stated. "You don't have to

waste your time with me anymore, because this case is done. Don't worry, I'll make sure to give excellent commendations to General Rouhr, I'm sure he'll be ecstatic to pin whatever medal you want on your chest."

She spat her last words and walked out the door.

MIRI

I left him, his room, his smug "I need my honor
back" attitude, and his lies. I had shared myself
with him, willingly, joyfully, oh god, so pleasurably, but
he had lied to me.

I'd just been a job. A means to an end.

I wasn't completely sure where to go. The only place
I could think of was back to my apartment. I didn't
want to go there, not with everything that had
happened and all the more recent bad memories, but I
guess my feet had decided for me. There I was, standing
in front of my apartment, trying to figure out if I
should go in or not.

"Hey, Miri," someone called from across the street in
a pleasant voice. I turned to see an older gentleman and
it only took a quick second to remember him.

"Hey, Mr. Horn. How are you?" I answered back with a wave.

He shrugged as best as he could as he used his cane to hold himself up while he reached down and pulled a small weed from his grass. "I'm doing well. Can't complain, at least not yet." I remembered that this was his standard response to everything. He was a good guy, I could trust that much.

Couldn't I?

"Well, if you find something to complain about, let me know," I shot back with a smile, my go-to response for him. He smiled, waved at me, and turned to go back into his tiny little house.

I took stock of my neighborhood. I looked up and down the street. Just, houses. On one side of the street were tiny little houses with their own yards, a small porch, and bright colors of paint. On the other side, my side, were bigger houses split in two to be used as duplexes. Not as bright on the coloring, but not bland, either. My place was the only one on the block that wasn't a duplex, it was a triplex and I had the middle one.

My neighbor to the right worked the overnight shift doing...something. I couldn't remember, but it didn't fill me with dread that I couldn't remember.

It was almost as if it was one of those things that I either never knew or never remembered in the first place, like someone's name when you meet them at a party and know you're never going to see them again, ever. My neighbor to the left wasn't even a neighbor, the place was empty.

The landlord hadn't rented it out in months, even after the reno had fixed the damage caused by the last tenant trying to use the place as a garage.

I was hesitating. I didn't want to go inside. I didn't want to be here, but where else was I supposed to go? I knew that Auntie had nothing to do with my kidnapping, but I still couldn't trust that her place was safe.

Why was it that the only man in my life that I could trust was old man Horn?

My hand was trembling as it hovered over the lock, key in hand.

Oh god, I remembered.

I hurried in, slamming and locking the door behind me, and rushed into the kitchen.

I remembered.

I moved to the fridge and reached for it, then stopped just short. Last time—the non-Zarik time—I'd been opening the fridge to get a bite to eat.

I had been hungry from cleaning. I thought I heard a truck pass by and it was louder than it should have been. I turned and saw that my door was open.

I wondered why it was open, then suddenly

something, no, some*one* hit me in the side of the head, wrapped their hand over my mouth and another over my eyes.

I kicked and fought, but another set of hands grabbed me as a rag was put over my nose and mouth, replacing the other hand. I shook my head and caught a small glimpse of a face before everything went dark.

Oh, my, god. Now I was hyperventilating, I couldn't breathe.

Kyle.

Kyle had been there.

He was the one that had knocked me unconscious with whatever was on that rag. That son of a bitch!

He had opened my door. He had let people into my home. He had been the one to KIDNAP ME! My mind was reeling, completely devastated by it. I thought I had been upset with him before, but to suddenly remember my own kidnapping and to remember that he was the one behind it, it was too much.

I ran to my bedroom, threw myself on my bed, and cried.

My cousin had betrayed me, tried to turn me into, into...

I stopped. What had he been trying to do? What had any of them been trying to do?

And why hadn't he been at that damn settlement with the rest of the bastards?

I jumped as something tapped my window. I saw the shadow of a bird through my curtains as it flew away. My heart, already racing from remembering, was nearly rocketing out of my chest. A loud truck rumbled by and I immediately dove under my bed, afraid that my door was open and that they were back.

I fought back tears and the panic that was threatening to take over. It was all done. It was all over. I was safe. Zarik had promi---

Then there was Zarik and his confession that he had jumped in to help me in order to regain his honor or some shit.

Why in the hell did he have to do that?

Another knock on my window sent me flying out of my bedroom and rushing into the kitchen. I grabbed the biggest knife I had and wheeled around, looking for my kidnapper. No one was there.

It was just me and a tree branch.

I forced a laugh just so I wouldn't panic again. I had to do something. "I need to replace the locks." My own voice was a bit startling to hear, but it was comforting, as well. I called a local locksmith, but he was busy on another call at the moment.

He wouldn't be here for a few hours.

A few more hours of just me, in a place where I had been stolen from, in a place where someone might have a spare key to get in.

Lovely.

Knife still in hand, I sat down on my tiny little couch and put on some music. If I stayed in the silence, I was going to lose my mind.

Not like I hadn't pretty nearly lost it already.

"This is screwed up," I said out loud, just to have someone talking. I had almost forgotten that my latest musical interest was a collection of instrumentals, so there were no lyrics. How in the hell did I ever decide that was a good thing?

I got up and messed with my music, putting on some stuff that had real sound and real words to it. "Much better," I said to no one in particular. "Oh yeah, sing to me, Luther. Take my stress away."

Okay, maybe talking to a dead musician wasn't the sanest thing in the world to do, but at least Luther wasn't going to betray me, use me, or try to kidnap me.

Then, I laughed at myself a little. I was doing something that Zarik and Kyle had both done.

I was putting my own needs first. I needed calm, so I put on music. Zarik needed to fix some bullshit honor-code thing, so he chose me. I mean, people will take care of themselves, right?

Kyle, well, I didn't want to think about that asshole, so I shifted back to Zarik. I was still sore from sleeping with him, but it was a good sore. I...I *liked* being this kind of sore.

"Dammit," I cursed quietly. "Why did he have to tell me that? Why did he have to say something and ruin the mystique?"

Remembering how he'd felt, I sank back into the couch and let out a small moan. God, he had felt so good.

His hands so gentle, his touch so loving, and his... "Oh, hell no, not this song." I got up and changed the song. It had been playing when I had been taken. I didn't want that song on, not now, at least.

How could Zarik have used me? Or, did he? I know he said he chose the assignment as a way of making up for what had happened in the past, but how he treated me and acted towards me, that was real. Wasn't it?

I know I definitely felt something and I'm not that much of an idiot to have mistaken his looks, his touches, and his tone when he was nice and gentle with me. He felt something for me. He honestly did. I might not know a damn thing about him, but there was no way he was that good of an actor.

Was he?

I missed him. I missed his giant hands that dwarfed mine. I missed the way his hands touched my shoulders with gentle power, how his hand easily fit on my back.

I missed the sound and tone of his voice when we joked and when he promised to take care of me.

I missed how he looked at me.

Could the idea of him trying to regain his honor really be that bad of a thing?

I knew that I still, still, still what? Did I love him?

Oh.

I sat up, knowing that if I had company, they would be weirded out by the look on my face. "It was real. He does want me and feel for me, just like I want him. I don't want this to be just something that happened. It was too good."

Oh, god it was, too. "I *feel* for this ridiculously tall man, and I know he feels for me, too."

I had to talk to him, but I also had to wait for the locksmith.

Damn.

ZARIK

I had always been told that truth was valuable, that truth was desired, and that truth was the correct path.

Whoever had said that neglected to mention that truth was also painful.

It didn't take long for Miri to leave after I told her the truth about why I had originally taken her case.

And I couldn't blame her.

To find out you had been used for something is gut-wrenching, and the fact that I'm the one that wrenched her gut made it that much worse, especially considering what we did last night.

Miri has to think that I used her there, as well.

I would if I were her.

But I didn't, and I didn't know how to go about convincing her of that.

And my sitting here in my room, sulking, was just a complete waste of time.

While I didn't have work to do at the moment, I could still find something to make myself useful.

So I headed upstairs to talk to Tobias, to see if he needed anything or knew of something I could do.

As I topped the stairs, I saw Hileen sitting in the lobby again. I felt bad for her. When I had brought Miri out to her, I saw the pain in her eyes when she saw that it wasn't her daughter being brought out.

Yet, here she was.

She wasn't giving up.

I shouldn't either.

Then, something dawned on me. There were women in the infirmary that had been taken, what if...I headed to Tobias.

"Tobias," I whispered as I came up next to him.

He jumped slightly, looked up at me, then let out a breath. "You scared me," he whispered back. "Why are we whispering?"

I nodded towards Hileen. "What was her daughter's name again? I don't have the file with me."

His eyes went wide with recognition and he quickly turned to his computer and typed something into it. Within a few seconds, he had her file open. "Her daughter's name is, hold on, Cora." Then he shot me another look. "One of the women you guys brought in is named Cora," he whispered excitedly. "Do you think it could be?"

"I hope so," I whispered to him. I quickly stood and raised my voice. "Ms. Hileen?"

She looked over at me, her eyes filled with a mixture of hope, expectation, and fear. "Yes?"

"Ma'am," I started as I walked over to her, "I don't mean to get your hopes up, but we found a," I hesitated a bit as I searched for the right information. "Yesterday, we found a hidden location of some humans trying to 're-educate' others against us. We found a couple young women there."

Her eyes began to well up a bit as she gasped. I just hoped that I was right this time. "If you would follow me, ma'am. I'm hoping we found your daughter this time." I held my hand out to her to help her stand, then led her to the infirmary. I walked her right by Dr. Parr, who looked at me oddly, then stood up and followed us.

"In here," I said quietly. Hileen walked through the double doors that I indicated, with Dr. Parr and me half a step behind.

She stood still for a moment, looking at the people inside, then her breath caught and her hand went up to her mouth while tears streamed down her cheeks.

I followed her gaze to the woman I had rescued

from the underground lab and I was forced to blink my own eyes clear.

"Cora?"

The young woman in the bed looked over and she let out an almost heartbroken sob as Hileen rushed over. Mother and daughter hugged and cried as they were finally reunited.

"You crying?"

I looked down at Dr. Parr, my vision blurry. I didn't bother replying as she leaned into me for a moment. "You did good."

I nodded. It felt good to finally reunite these two. Miri would have loved it. I suddenly felt bad for her not being here and decided that I needed to apologize and do whatever it took to convince her that I truly did miss her and care for her.

"Excuse me, doctor," I said as I turned and left the room, Hileen and Cora's joy filling my ears.

I decided to go to Miri's apartment. I had to try again. And again, if that's what it took.

I was almost out of the hospital when I received a call on my comm. Hoping it was Miri, I looked down and was unable to hide my disappointment when I saw that it was Leena instead.

"What can I do for you?" I answered.

"Hey, I know this isn't usually your field, but since

you were the one that found all of this, I thought you'd want to see it," was her response.

"What would that be?"

"Just come to my lab, please," she requested. "It's easier to show you." She ended the call, leaving me to wonder what she was talking about.

I went to her lab. "What's going on?" I asked as I walked into her lab. I possibly should have knocked as two of Leena's assistants jumped and glared at me for interrupting their work. I held up my hands in an apologetic manner and made my way to Leena's desk. "What's going on?" I repeated, a little more quietly.

She flashed me a quick smile and pointed at the datapads that I had confiscated from the idiots. "Daphne's hacker friend has been super helpful in getting into the rest of these. I was looking into the datapads to see what they had done in regard to their synthetic memory-erasing compound, and I found some serious shit." I was a bit taken aback by her candor. She had never spoken to me like this before. Maybe I wasn't as faceless as I used to be. Maybe I never had been. "They were really intense with what they were doing."

She grabbed one of the pads that was still on and swiped to a file she had open. "Here," she said, handing it to me. "What you'll find there is essentially a memorandum written up by their leader, detailing their overall objective. They were trying to essentially re-wire people's minds to make them think that you guys were here to destroy all of us."

"We already knew that," I said.

She nodded. "Yeah, but what you didn't know was that this is a massive operation and that they were in the testing phase. They were taking anyone, even if that meant people kidnapping their own family," she gave me a look.

Like Miri, taken by her cousin's friend.

"They've already tested this on over a dozen people, each time making the serum more potent and effective." She reached up and swiped to another file, a large list of names. "This is the list of the people involved, or that *want* to be involved. There's a massive population that doesn't like you guys, or those of us that do like you," she added.

"We already knew that," I countered. It didn't seem plausible that every human would like us, or even come around to tolerating us.

Intolerance was a standard option in living beings. Most people were better at ignoring their intolerance than others. Something didn't sit with me, however. Leena looked stressed. "But this isn't what's stressing you out, is it?"

She shook her head. "No. This is," she reached over and grabbed another datapad, a large silver one that she had connected to her computer. "I was looking through this one after receiving the decrypted the files and I'm not happy with what I've found. They have intimate knowledge of the Puppet Master; what he is, what he does, basically they know almost everything we know about him."

That was bad. Detailed knowledge of the Puppet Master wasn't supposed to be public. People knew of him, and had basic ideas of what he was capable of, but this kind of information had been held back. I scrolled through the files that Leena already had open and they were in depth, highly detailed files about the Puppet Master.

"But how did they get this information?" I asked.

She shrugged and shook her head. "I don't have a clue. We've got a hacker on our side. It's not that far of a stretch that they have one, too. One more thing…"

I looked at her.

"They know where he is and how to get to him," she said.

Rek!

"Have you shown any of this to the general?" I asked.

"Parts of it," she answered. "I just decoded this info as you were walking over."

This was distressing to say the least. "Thank you,

Leena. I'll notify the general right away. Can you send a copy of these files to his tablet?"

I waved her off as I left her lab at a light jog.

Within moments, I was in Rouhr 's office. He had Leena on speaker and between the two of us, we explained Leena's findings and what my suggestion was.

"Good call, Leena," he said as he punched up the barracks and ordered the strike teams to mobilize. "You, too," he said with a nod in my direction. I nodded as well and rushed out to the barracks and the armory.

As I rushed out, I couldn't stop worrying.

Not about the Puppet Master. We were doing everything we could. It would have the best protection on the planet.

But this delayed my conversation with Miri. With every step away, I wanted to pull back to her side.

I just hoped she would understand.

I needed her to understand.

That might finally make this pain in my chest go away.

MIRI

The lock was installed, my mind was slightly more at ease, and I had a meeting with Dr. Parr. Steps. Nice, tangible steps, that didn't involve me hiding under the bed with a knife.

I decided that I would take a cab, not really feeling like walking that far to her office.

That rift thing was useful. But way too cold.

And still a little weird.

When the cab pulled up, I got in and made myself comfortable.

"Hospital, please," I said to the cabbie. He nodded and started driving. He tried to strike up a conversation with me, but I was too preoccupied thinking about Zarik.

I tried to force him from my mind so I could make

sure to remember what I needed to talk to Evie about.

I needed to ask her about the memories that were suddenly returning, especially the more traumatic ones. I wanted to make sure that the brain scans were okay and that the sudden return of my bad memories weren't messing me up.

The problem was, trying to force Zarik out of my mind was something that was messing me up. I couldn't think straight.

Every time I tried to force my concentration, I saw his smile, or heard his voice trying to encourage me and push me. All I succeeded in doing in my attempt to not think about Zarik was to think about him even more.

"We're here, lady." I looked up to see that the cabbie was pulling into the hospital parking lot. He hovered in front of the hospital as I paid him and got out.

He sped off, leaving me to wonder if I had upset him or something. Just because I didn't want to talk didn't mean that I had an issue with him, I just didn't want to talk.

What was wrong with that?

Then, I looked back up at the hospital and realized that I was in the wrong place. I was at the hospital like I was supposed to be, but Evie's office was on the *other* side.

Steps. Just more tangible ones.

Resigning myself to a short hike around the

hospital, I started walking. The more steps I took, the harder it was for me to take my mind off Zarik. I wondered what he was doing and if he was angry with me.

I had stormed off. I had left him and been angry with him. I wouldn't be surprised if he didn't want to see me, not after how angry I had gotten.

I wanted to talk to him, to tell him that I forgave him. I knew that he didn't mean to hurt me, and that his need to make up for part of his past was important to him. I wanted to tell him that I understood, and that he also needed to not let his past control him anymore.

Then again, if I was being honest, if it hadn't been for him trying to make up for whatever mistakes he had made in the past, we would never have met and I might not have ever figured out what happened to me.

I might have fallen by the wayside and merely become another one of those people just trying to somehow make it through life, maybe without ever getting my memories back.

I guess him doing what he did for the reasons that he did them ended up being a good thing, in a sort of convoluted way.

Right?

I rounded the corner of the hospital and spotted Zarik and the rest of the soldiers he had told me were strike team members. They were in full gear and marching with determination back towards the offices. Letting my curiosity get the better of me, I rushed over.

"Zarik," I called out with a big wave of my arm. I saw him look around to see where his name had come from, finally spotting me. He stopped as I caught up. "What's going on?" I asked, a bit out of breath.

He didn't even hesitate in his answer. "Leena's team managed to crack the security on the datapads that I found. She's discovered that the anti-alien group has more in-depth knowledge of the Puppet Master than previously believed, including its location. We're on our way there now to make sure things are safe and to set up a defensive perimeter, just in case."

I took a minute to soak up what he told me. If the group knew about the Puppet Master's location, and if the Puppet Master was what Zarik had told me it was, if the group killed it, that would mean the planet would die. Right?

"I'm going with you," I said impulsively, not recognizing my own voice at first.

When I saw his surprise, and felt that my own face mirrored his surprise, I set my jaw and folded my arms in front of me. I was determined to not be left behind.

He put his hand on my shoulder. "No," he said as I grabbed his hand. I looked at him as if he had spoken in a foreign language.

"What do you mean, 'no'?" I asked. He looked at me

and I could see the honest to goodness care and worry in his eyes. I never so badly wanted to hug anyone and hold anyone as closely as I wanted to hold him at that moment.

"You can't come with us," he said, a bit of force behind his words.

I tilted my head as I looked at him. I pushed his hand off of my shoulder and changed my look into a glare. "Really? You don't want me there?"

He shook his head. "It might not be safe there," he said. Then, before I could answer, he left to catch up with the others.

I chased after him, my thoughts racing with my feet. Everything lately felt like a choice had been made for me. Getting grabbed by Kyle. Their stupid experiments. Staying in the holding cell. Zarik and his honor and whatever was growing between us.

I was making this decision on my own, even if it wasn't particularly well thought out, damn it.

I saw the rift opening a few yards away and turned on the speed. I raced past Zarik, who was trying to reach out for me, and jumped through the rift. The cold was unbearable, but since I had jumped through, it was quick.

I landed on dirt, sticking my arms out to catch myself. The rift set me down in front of a tunnel that led down.

"What are you doing?" I heard from behind me. I didn't even have to turn around to know that Zarik had followed me through and was angry.

Whoops.

I turned around, a big smile on my face. "You couldn't stop me. Big bad you couldn't stop little bitty me. That's funny."

I could see the corners of his mouth trying to tug their way upwards, but he fought the smile that I knew he wanted to show. The General Rouhr and the others came through the rift, and as the last one came through, a big orange and red behemoth that wasn't as tall as Zarik but was so much wider than him, the rift closed.

"You mind explaining this, Zarik?" one of the soldiers asked. I guessed that by the way Zarik looked at him, this guy was one of the leaders.

While Zarik talked to the others, I turned around and walked a few yards down the tunnel to the opening where I could see the Puppet Master.

"Hello, child," I heard in my head. That was, by far, the weirdest part of all of this. The fact that he was a giant flower hanging from the ceiling by dozens of vines seemed par for the course, considering all the aliens that have been on the planet lately. This whole talking into my head thing was just flat-out odd.

"My apologies, young Miri. My ability to use what you call normal *verbal communication was something that left*

my kind many generations ago as we evolved," he explained to me. *"Now, what can I do for you today?"*

I found myself trembling, but when I tried to talk, the words seemed to just tumble out of my mouth. "I wanted to thank you for fixing my memory," I started, then stopped in embarrassment. How could I tell a being such as this that I was grateful for him fixing my memory?

"I believe you just did," came the voice in my mind, a mental chuckle resonating in my brain. *"Please do not feel uncomfortable around me, I promise that I will not harm you,"* he said.

"I'll try," I answered. "It's just a little weird to be talking to a massive plant that happens to be the life-force behind a planet, you know?"

"Then please imagine my initial awkwardness trying to speak with tiny creatures that were living on me," he said back, a bit of humor injecting itself into my mind to let me know he was joking.

"Fair point," I conceded.

"And here I was, getting used to being the biggest one around." Zarik came up behind me, his hand resting gently on my shoulder, sending shivers up and down my body as I remembered what those hands had done to me, as well as the double entendre of the word *biggest.*

"I must apologize for our barging into your lair,"

Zarik said to the Puppet Master.

"*I understand,*" came the answer for us all to hear. I guessed. "*Young Miri's mind was racing a bit as she rushed through the rift and I was able to decipher your purpose.*"

Zarik nodded and flashed me an encouraging smile. "Then you know that, somehow, this anti-alien faction of humans knows where you are."

"*Yes.*"

"Well, we're here to offer you our protection, if that is satisfactory," Zarik said. He had not quite mastered the political decorum that General Rouhr had, but he was close.

When I'd jumped through the rift, I hadn't expected to be so close to being bored and disappointed.

I learned a lot from speaking with the Puppet Master, but I was disappointed. Not disappointed that nothing happened, that was good.

But I was a bit disappointed that Zarik and I were surrounded by the rest of the strike teams and had no time to speak.

Just as I tried to get Zarik off to the side, a strange noise floated down the tunnels.

"*They are here,*" the Puppet Master said. "They have carved a separate path than the one I created for your rift. They have been very intent on finding me."

I was suddenly terrified.

Not bored at all.

ZARIK

They streamed into the cavernous hall like a raging river, angry voices bouncing off the walls and blending in with the thud of heavy boots stomping the stony ground.

They had found a way towards the Puppet Master that didn't involve us.

I was starting to shake my head, wondering exactly how resourceful these humans were. It didn't make sense. There had to be something more driving them than pure hatred. In my experience, the humans were technologically backward - for them to accomplish all that they had to drive a wedge between our peoples and attack the Puppet Master, someone had to be guiding them.

But who?

And why?

The answer would not come now. But it was something I'd have to bring up to the general at a later date. After my actions here, I hoped that he would include me in matters that involved the Puppet Master.

I held my rifle tightly, resting my index finger on the trigger as I took aim. The man in my crosshairs couldn't be older than thirty, but his unkempt hair and dirty clothes made him look much older than he really was.

He held an old rifle in his hands, but his hands started shaking the moment he realized I was aiming at him.

Looking to the sides, I gritted my teeth as I saw more and more of the humans stepping into the cavern. There were way more people than I assumed would be necessary to collect the toxin, and they were all heavily armed. Despite their ragtag appearance, they also seemed more than eager to fight. Hopefully it wouldn't come to that...if anyone opened fire in these caverns, we'd have a bloodbath in our hands.

And with the Puppet Master thrown into the mix, who knew what could happen?

"Easy now," I said, but that just hardened the expression of the man I was watching.

"Lay down your weapons!" General Rouhr shouted, his voice echoing throughout the cavern. Some men took a few steps back, but the majority stood their ground. Finally, one of them stepped forward, an angry expression in his face.

"You don't get to boss us around, you filthy scum," he said, and then spat on the ground. I immediately turned so I had him in my crosshairs.

"That's right!" another man shouted. "You fuckin' aliens are done. We're not your fuckin' servants."

I took a few seconds to assess the situation, and that was enough for me to realize most of the group hadn't been expecting to see any of us in here.

Most of them were young, and they seemed extremely nervous and agitated. They weren't expecting a confrontation, and now their ringleaders were trying to put on a show to reassure the group.

"Why don't we *all* put our weapons down?" I tried to say. I didn't like the situation one bit, especially because Miri had insisted on tagging along. If anything happened to her, I would never forgive myself. "There's no reason for any of this."

"Is that right, huh?" the man in front of the group asked, flashing me a toothy grin. "I think there are mighty fucking reasons for this, you fucking monster. You don't belong here, none of you do...and the same goes for that fucking thing!" Pointing toward the Puppet Master, he then spat onto the ground once more. The situation was slowly spiraling out of control, and I had to find a way to stop it.

"You don't know what you're saying," I insisted. "That *thing* there is the beating heart of the whole planet. It's what holding the planet together. More than that, it is a friend...of *everyone*."

"Bullshit!"

"No, it's not—"

"Of course it's bullshit!" the man shouted, pacing back and forth in front of his group. "Why don't you just tell us the truth? Why don't you admit that fucking thing is one of your creations? You're using it to kill the planet faster, so that you can crush us under your heels!" Turning around so that he was facing his group, he thumped his chest with his fist. "But we won't stand for it! We will defend our planet! WHATEVER IT FUCKING TAKES!"

His rebel army cried out its agreement, and I let out a small sigh.

There was no stopping this bloodbath.

As the man wheeled around once more, I gritted my teeth as I saw him raise his rifle in the general's direction. Before he could squeeze the trigger, though, I opened fire and hit him dead center, his chest caving in with the force of the impact.

Then it was chaos.

Everyone started firing at the same time, and the

cavern was lit up by gunfire. There were screams, some born out of courage, others out of panic and pain. The humans tried to look for cover, hiding behind whatever rock formation was in their way, but our strike teams were too fast for them.

We flanked them in the blink of an eye, carefully shooting down the more dangerous elements and subduing those who decided to surrender.

I paused for a moment, my heart thumping in my ears, and scanned the cavern with a quick glance. *Where are you, Miri?* I thought, panic slowly swamping me. I finally noticed her in one of the corners, a wall of vines in front of her.

It seemed like the General had been right: the Puppet Master really had a soft spot for human females.

"You're fucking dead!" I heard someone shout behind me, and I turned around to face another of the humans. He was staring at me, a murderous look in his eyes, and he squeezed the trigger on his rifle.

Skrell!

For a moment, I thought that was it. I would die here, in this cavern, and everything I still wanted to do with Miri...nothing but dreams carried away by the wind. I would never have a second chance with her, and I would die knowing that she hated me for what I had done.

There'd be no redemption for me.

Only then did I notice that his rifle had misfired.

Before he could aim and make another try, I simply launched myself and struck him in the stomach with my right shoulder.

We crashed onto the ground together, his rifle flying through the hair in a wild arc, and I immediately tried to punch him. He moved his head to the side and I missed my target, my fist smashing against the rocky ground.

He tried to strike back by headbutting me, but I reacted fast: using my free hand, I stretched my fingers wide and grabbed his head before it could connect with my nose. "Don't even think about it," I growled, punching his stomach so hard the man's eyes rolled in their sockets. He stopped moving a split-second later, unconscious.

Dusting myself off, I rose to my feet and looked around the cavern once more. Most of the humans had already surrendered their weapons, and those that hadn't were on the ground, either dead or unconscious.

Still, there weren't as many casualties as I had expected.

For that, we had to thank the Puppet Master. Instead of being idle, he used his vines to restrain some of the humans, whipping their guns out of their hands as the battle raged.

General Rouhr looked like he was busy talking with

the Puppet Master, but there was something that needed to be handled sooner than that.

"HQ, come in," I said into my comm between hard breaths, adrenaline still raging through my blood. "We're going to need reinforcements ASAP. We met hostiles in the caverns, and we don't know if there are more coming this way. Either way, we're going to need more people to haul all the prisoners out of here. Over."

"Copy that," HQ replied.

Wiping the sweat off my brow with the back of my hand, I leaned against one of the walls as I tried to catch my breath.

Miri! My heart rate shot up once more. Where was she? I looked to the place where she was, hiding behind a wall of vines, and I sighed audibly as I realized she was unharmed.

Now all I needed to do was prove I wasn't the asshole she now thought I was.

But that would mean bringing her into a part of my life that even I had run away from.

As the humans liked to say, easier said than done.

MIRI

I had panicked. This was a stupid decision. There were so many other ways I could have chosen to assert my free will.

I could have gotten a pet. I could have moved.

But no. I'd insisted on coming here.

Now I'd had nowhere to hide, and while no one was shooting directly at me, there were a few stray shots that had come close.

I dove to the ground and covered my head, then started to feel it rumbling beneath and around me. I uncovered my head to see a wall of vines weaving themselves together around me.

"Have no fear, young Miri. You shall always be protected around me," the Puppet Master said, the intensity of his

voice making it sound like he was speaking directly to me.

Through a few small holes in the vine wall, I watched as the fight continued. Thankfully, it didn't last too long and things ended quickly when alien and human soldiers began pouring through another rift, surrounding the anti-alien group. I saw that there were a few of the group being held by some vines.

"Couldn't resist hanging a few upside down, huh?" I said quietly, knowing the Puppet Master heard me.

A slight chuckle filled my mind as the three 'rebels' that were being held by their ankles were shaken a bit before being unceremoniously dropped to the ground. I laughed.

When things were clear, the vines were moved away from me. "Thank you," I said quietly as I patted one of the vines. I rushed to Zarik, remembering how he looked when he fought and remembering how that powerful body of his had felt underneath me.

Oh, how I wanted to feel it there again. I nearly tackled him as he turned at the sound of my running feet. I quickly kissed him on his cheek, then started checking him over for injuries.

"What are you doing?" he asked, failing miserably at hiding his amusement.

I looked up at him, a hand on my hip. "I didn't think it was that hard to figure out. I'm trying to see if you're hurt, but if you're one of those 'tough guys' that doesn't need a woman, I think there's a few of the guards over there looking this way. I can always, ahem, check them for injuries." I flashed him a sly grin as I said that and I was pleased to see his bone-white cheeks flush a little.

"No," he croaked. He cleared his throat, then spoke again. "No," he repeated. "I'm not one of those, um, guys. You may check me for injuries."

I slapped him on the chest, which was useless since he was wearing armor, but made me feel better. I finished checking him out, and having found nothing, I declared him fit and healthy.

"Does this mean you forgive me?" he asked after a moment of the two of us smiling at one another.

God, to look at him smiling at me, I loved it. I discovered that I craved that smile more than I craved chocolate, and I was addicted to that, especially chocolate-covered hazelnuts.

His question needed an answer, though.

Of course I forgave him. He had made a decision, and it had led to the two of us coming together, in more ways than one.

From the beginning, he had treated me with kindness and respect, and had been there for me when I had no one.

He supported me and took care of me and legitimately cared for me. Yes, he neglected to tell me something and he neglected it on purpose, but I understood why.

He was afraid of my reaction, the exact reaction that I'd given him.

I looked into his eyes and saw the fear, and it wasn't fear of dying, but fear of losing me. I was desperate to make sure he never had that fear again.

I nodded. "Of course," I said. "I'm not happy that you lied to me, and before you say anything," I said quickly, holding up my hand to stop him from talking, "you kept something from me, so you lied by omission, and that counts. But," I reached out and grabbed his hand, "I understand why you did it. So, of course I forgive you. Why wouldn't I?"

There was a look in his eyes, a hunger that took me by surprise, a hunger that, surprisingly, I felt for him in return. He didn't say a word, just grabbed me by the waist, tossed me in the air, and caught me when we were face-to-face.

He planted those incredible lips of his on mine and I lost all thought of everything but his lips and his body.

I wrapped my legs around him and kissed him back with a fervor that I didn't know I had. His tongue danced with mine as he squeezed me, while my hands ran across his bald head and down to his massive, toned shoulders.

It took a few moments, but then outside noises finally started to register in my brain.

"Fuckin' whore." "Disgusting." "Slut." "...down odds she sucks his dick right here, the fuckin' bitch," all came from the human throats while a few nervous coughs came from others.

I pulled away from Zarik, feeling the blood rush from my loins to my cheeks. "Um," I said hesitantly. Zarik looked around, a bit of red in his own cheeks as he set me down.

I looked around, then was suddenly slapped in the brain.

Not far away, Kyle, that asshole cousin of mine that had kidnapped me and tried to screw up my brain, was glaring at me in disgust.

I stomped my way over to him, a smug grin across my face.

"What do you want?" he growled. He tried to turn away from me, but the big guy holding him—I think his name was Axtin—yanked him back to face me.

I nodded a 'thank you' to Axtin, then stared at my cousin. "Why?"

He seemed surprised by my question. He started laughing. "To avoid seeing you whore yourself out like this," he spat. "Then again, that's all you ever were, weren't you?"

He opened his mouth to say more, but I was no

longer interested. My foot snapped out and caught him right in the groin.

He dropped to his knees, a girly scream emanating from his lips, mixing with the sympathetic groan from several of the men around, including Axtin, who still managed to flash me an approving smile. "You'll be a good mate, little one."

I leaned down and grabbed my cousin by the hair, forcing his face up so he could see me. "You're an idiot. Did you know that every single one of these non-humans, their human friends, and even *him*," I said, emphasizing my point by pointing at the Puppet Master, "they all have more humanity in them than you do? At least they wouldn't betray and kidnap their own family, and for what? Some idiotic scheme to fuck up our brains and make us all think like you?" I spat on the ground in front of him. "God, you are so fucking stupid."

"Fuck you," he cursed through clenched teeth. "You're just an alien-fucking whore."

I shrugged. "Eh, believe what you want. At least I don't have to worry about being hurt by them, not like I do with my so-called family. So, if you wanna think of me as some sort of whore, fine, go ahead." I stood up, dropping his head.

I glared down at him as he tried to look at me in defiance. "I'll spend my life being a *happy* 'alien-fucking whore'." I turned around, fully intent on leaving it at that, but something in the back of my head said that one more thing was needed.

I heard Axtin pull Kyle to his feet, and I spun around and gave as hard a kick as I could, my foot connecting with Kyle's ribs. A crack filled the air, along with the *whumph* of the air rushing from his lungs. I kicked him, again, in his tiny little crotch, then turned from him and walked away.

Zarik was struggling to hold back his smile while I heard several members of the strike teams laughing. A few of the human guards were mumbling, but I could tell they were proud of me.

The grin on my face was from ear to ear, and I truly enjoyed how sore my cheeks felt because of that grin.

"Ready to go?" I asked Zarik as I walked up to him, holding my hand out for his.

"That was impressive. Didn't know you could kick that well," he commented as he took my hand. "I mean, I knew your legs were strong, but, that," he jutted his chin out towards Kyle, "that looked like fun."

I had to admit, it really was. "I didn't know I could, until I had the urge," I teased. "Now I gotta wash his stink off me," I said with genuine disgust.

Zarik leaned down to talk to me only. "I can help you with that," he offered.

"Ooh. Fun."

With an amused shake of his head, General Rouhr yelled out orders to all the others before calling for a rift to be opened. You know, I was determined to figure out who this Fen character was. I wanted to get to know *everyone* that Zarik knew.

With a gentle squeeze of his hand, I pulled him towards the rift so we could go home.

ZARIK

I had been called to the general's office. He didn't tell me why, just left a message for me to come to his office an hour after sunrise. So, there I was, sitting on the bench outside his office, waiting, and thinking.

Two days ago, we had arrested a large number of humans that had attempted to attack the Puppet Master. They had wanted to somehow get its secretion that affected memory. They were trying to create their own synthetic compound to erase the memories of other humans so they could convince them that we were the evil ones, here to kill all humans.

We've bled, killed, and had a few of our own killed to protect them and get rid of the Xathi threat.

We blew up our own ship and dismantled another ship to help fix things here.

But still, some people couldn't see that.

Some people, all they saw was the difference in our races, or species, or whatever they saw when they looked at us.

There had been terrible wars between Valorni, Skotan, and K'ver peoples, many times simply because someone didn't like the way someone else talked, or looked, or for what they believed.

So, now that I was on the receiving end of the asinine bigotry and hatred, I understood how my own bigotry and hatred were stupid. That still didn't excuse it, though.

I sat there, trying to take my mind off all of that and focus on something else. Luckily, I had the perfect distraction.

Miri.

She was an incredible woman that did things for me, and to me, that I had never thought I deserved.

I had made mistakes, mistakes that had cost an entire family their lives, and those were mistakes that I would never be able to escape.

However, thanks to Miri, I now realized that I no longer had to atone for those mistakes to regain my honor. I simply had to learn from them in order to keep focused and not make the same mistakes again.

Footsteps from down the hall brought me back to reality. I looked up to see Tobias walking to his desk in the lobby as he tossed a wave in my direction. I waved back, then stood as the general rounded the corner.

"Sir," I said with a salute as the general came close.

"Easy," he said with a smile. "Come in." He opened his office and ushered me in. "Take a seat," he offered, indicating the chair in front of his desk. I sat down, still wondering what this was all about.

He poured himself a glass of water, raising his eyebrow in question at me. I shook my head. With a shrug, he sat down in his chair, took a quick drink, then took in a deep breath. "I'm going to assume you're wondering what this is all about. Am I right?"

I nodded.

"Good," he said with a smile. "I was wanting to keep you in suspense a little bit, figured you deserved the stress after what you've done the last few days."

Now I was really confused. As far as I knew, the last few days were good work by me. Why would I deserve stress? My face must have shown my confusion.

Rouhr grinned, almost cruelly. "It's alright. I'm having a bit of fun at your expense. I brought you here to tell you that I am very proud of what you've done."

"Thank you, sir," I said with trepidation. I was still confused.

"You take good news so well," he said sarcastically. He put his hands in front of his face, let out a deep breath, then stood. "Follow me."

He led me over to the couch, motioning for me to sit in one of the more comfortable chairs while he sat on the couch. "You surprised me when you volunteered to take this assignment. I wasn't sure what you were up to, but you were convincing.

"To be honest, sir," I cut in, "it wasn't terribly hard. I knew that not many of the others would have wanted to deal with an amnesiac girl, so I was trying to do you a favor. You would have had too many of the others complain."

"Hmm, you're not wrong," he admitted. "Most of them would have probably considered this as something beneath them. Which is why I'm grateful to you for stepping up. You took on something that should have been beneath you, that should have been assigned to one of the guards.

"But, since you took it on, you went beyond the call of duty." He grinned at me again. "A little further than beyond, but that's another story."

"Ha. Ha," I said flatly in response to his joke.

He smiled. "Look, what I'm trying to say is that you performed admirably and beyond your duties. You did more than was asked and, in the process, you uncovered something that would have been devastating to all of us if you hadn't."

"I'm sure we would have..." I started.

"Found it all out?" he interrupted. "When? When it

was too late to do anything? Or how about when they attacked the Puppet Master and harmed him? You're right, we *might* have found out in time, but we might not have. With your actions, your determination, and your insatiable drive to try to prove yourself, you ended up taking this further. It was that action that gave us what we needed to shut down a potential catastrophe."

He leaned forward on the couch and fitted me with a hard stare. "Listen, you may not feel that what you did was important, but it was, and not only to me or Miri."

That caught my attention. "What do you mean, sir?"

"You saved Miri's life. You worked hard to help her regain her memories, and you were there when she had a panic attack when she *did* remember them," the general said. He leaned back on the couch. "You pushed, you prodded, you were there when information was found, you were there when information was deciphered, you were the one that found the underground lab. So," he said, holding up a finger to quash my forthcoming comments. "Because of all that, I wanted to tell you something."

He reached into his pocket and pulled out a small piece of paper. "This paper, if we were anywhere near the rest of our kind and near proper military channels, would be my recommendation for you to receive the Silver Crystal."

I was stunned. The Silver Crystal was one of the

highest honors a soldier could receive. He was recommending me for that? I couldn't breathe.

He leaned forward again. "You stepped up, and you did things that resulted in our safety and, if not a shut-down, then a serious slow-down of this anti-alien group's agenda. You saved lives, you stopped a rebellion, and you acted phenomenally. You earned it."

"Th-th-thank you, sir," I stuttered out. I was flabbergasted by what he was telling me.

"Now, I have a question for you," he said.

"Yes, sir?"

"Do you want the official ceremony that is traditional for an award such as this?"

And there it was, my snap back to reality. I was being honored for something. I had done something well, very well, and I had somehow fixed things.

"I'm proud of you, as are the others. You deserve this," he was saying.

That was all I needed. I didn't need the pomp and circumstance of everything. The rest of them knew I was worthy but, more importantly, Miri knew I was worthy and so did I. Maybe I hadn't made up for my past mistakes, but I had certainly made things better.

"No, sir," I said. He seemed a bit confused, so I clarified. "I don't need the ceremony, sir. I don't want it. Your recognition, as well as my own improved belief in myself, is all I need. Thank you, sir."

I stood up, shook his hand, assured him that I was okay without the ceremony, and he smiled. "Very well. I approve," he said. "If you don't want the ceremony, then we won't have it. I'm proud of you, and I back your decision. Go, enjoy your day off with Miri."

"Yes, sir," I said happily.

That was certainly something I could do.

MIRI

"Mmph." That wasn't exactly what I wanted to say when Zarik got out of the bed, but I had my hair in my mouth.

"My, aren't you the articulate one?" he cracked as he pulled his pants up, taking away my beautiful view of his nakedness.

My disappointment in that actually hurt my chest. Wow, and to think, two weeks ago I was just a normal human girl with a job and—oh, shit. I had a job. Damn. Not sure I'm going to have that anymore. Oh, well. Where was I? Oh, yeah, staring at his incredibly toned body.

"Well, when you have a mouthful of hair, it's a little difficult to make a coherent sound," I explained.

"Oh, so what was your excuse last night?" he smiled at me.

"AH!" I gasped. I threw a pillow at him. "You are such an ass!"

He caught the pillow and came back over to me. He leaned over and kissed me on the head. "You love that, too," he teased, then smacked me playfully with the pillow.

"Ha. What are you getting dressed for?" I asked as I sat up, the sheet barely covering me.

"I got a message to meet General Rouhr first thing."

Now I was a little worried. "What about? Did he say? Is everything alright?"

He chuckled as he pulled on his shirt. "I'll find out in just a few."

That had been our conversation this morning before he left.

He had gone early, which wasn't terribly hard, he lived in a tiny-ass room in the basement of the office building.

If he had ever been late to a meeting, I wasn't sure how.

I occupied myself with getting some breakfast, then sitting in his room messing around on his datapad. I looked up the news, checked my messages, started looking up jobs, and just essentially trying to spend my time *not* thinking about what could possibly be happening upstairs.

I mean, was he giving Zarik another mission? Was that mission going to be dangerous? Was there a chance that I could lose him right after I just got him?

Oh god, what if that was it?

What if he was being sent away on a mission that was super deadly? I started panicking, my breathing coming in short, rapid bursts as my palms started to sweat and I started to just freak out.

My vision started to blur as I sat there and pictured all the terrible things that could happen to that behemoth of a man that I had found and fallen in love with.

I needed to calm down. I forced my breathing to slow, to deepen, to go back to normal. He was a good soldier, he was a survivor, and he was careful.

I had to understand that he was going to be sent out on missions on occasion, and that they would be dangerous. I was going to worry about him, but I had to trust in him, in his skills, and in his ability to live.

I'd seen him fight. He'd be unstoppable.

I dragged another lungful of air in.

Still shaky.

Of course, he might not be getting a mission right now. He might have just been called into the general's office to give a report or something.

Yeah, that was it.

He was just doing his job and everything was going to be fine.

I just had to believe that.

Two hours after he left, he came back. Two hours of me trying to occupy myself and driving myself into a momentary panic, and he came back with a look of complete shock and joy on his face.

"What happened?" I asked as he came in. I wrapped my arms around him, determined to make him feel better if this was bad news...or to make myself feel better if it was bad-for-me news.

He wrapped his big arms around me and bent himself down to kiss the top of my head. "Uh," he started to say, then his body shook a bit.

I looked up at him, scared, but when I looked into his eyes, I saw pride, joy, elation, and a measure of accomplishment that I hadn't seen before. He was shaking from excitement and happiness.

"What?" I asked.

He looked down at me and I saw the beginnings of a tear welling up in his left eye. "I," he looked away from me, then looked back. "I went upstairs."

"Uh huh," I said, trying to prod him on.

"General Rouhr gave me the Silver Crystal," he said reverently. "That's the highest military honor a soldier could receive without dying. He said he was proud of me." His voice started to break only slightly before it regained its strength. "The men congratulated me, Rouhr is proud of me, and I did things right."

I pulled him close, holding onto him as hard as I could. I was so happy for him. "You're amazing, love. You are."

He pulled away and looked down at me. "I couldn't have done it without you," he said, his voice husky. "You gave me something I thought that I had lost many years ago."

"What?"

"There's a sense of compassion and emotional connection that I have with you, that I have with others now, because of you," he told me. "If it wasn't for you, I'd still be locked up in my head here, obsessing about my honor."

"And now you're down here, sharing this insanely small room with me," I said sort of perky-like. He smiled.

"Yes, that I am." He leaned down and kissed me, hard. "I like that."

"I do, too. You saved me, Zarik," I said, wrapping my arms around his neck and letting him pick me up. "You saved me from death, from being part of that shit my cousin was involved with. You gave me life, Zarik. I love you."

He cocked his head to the side a bit, then smiled. "I love you, too," he said.

He planted a kiss on my cheek, then trailed kisses down the line of my neck until he reached the neckline of my blouse. His hands reached for mine, and our fingers laced with one another, held on top of my head. He held my hands there with one hand and unbuttoned my blouse with the other. Then he explored my exposed skin, trailing his fingers from my stomach up to my collarbone as he backed me toward the bed and lowered me to the mattress.

"I love you more," I whispered back, and stretched to kiss him again.

I slowly opened my legs around him as he settled in between my thighs. I could feel his cock pulsating inside his pants as he pressed against my wet core. His lips left my mouth, made their way to my breasts, and feasted on my nipples.

He flicked them around with his tongue, soliciting moans from my pleasured body, while he slowly ground his hips against mine. I continued to moan, the fabric covering my pussy was getting wetter by the moment. My hands grasped at his back, trying my best to tempt and entice him.

It seemed to work, as I felt his cock stiffen even harder against me. He took off his uniform, leaving nothing but his pants, that I unzipped with fumbling hands. I tugged at them, pulling them down to his knees together with his boxers, and revealed his massive cock.

It sprung out of its confinement, its head teasing the wet folds of my pussy. Zarik grabbed it with one hand and rubbed it hard against my mound. I let out another series of moans as my body tingled with the immense pleasure spreading all throughout.

He finally pulled down my panties and positioned his head between my legs.

"W-What are you doing?" I asked, my head fazed from all the sensations.

"I'm hungry," he said.

He didn't give me enough time to reply. Instead, he spread my legs even wider with his strong hands, pushing me down on the bed as his tongue licked my very center. I arched my back, my loud moans filling the small room.

He continued to play with my small button of pleasure and nibbled gently on it, which again sent waves of lust from my legs up to my head.

Suddenly, he broke away and moved into position on top of me. He grabbed his cock again and placed the tip inside my slick entrance.

I held on to his back with every push, and he got another inch of his cock inside my pussy. He pushed it again one more time, my hips arched higher to receive him, and, with one last thrust, he managed to fit his huge cock into my small and quaking body.

"Oh, God," I moaned, my body felt so full of him as he filled every inch of my pussy.

"Are you alright?" he asked and kissed my forehead.

I nodded and kissed him back. "I want more of you."

He smiled down at me and started thrusting. I gasped at the feel of him shoving his shaft through my wet folds.

Zarik panted above me, with his mouth near my ear to let me know how much he delighted in making love with me. I held my arms around his back, and with the little strength that I had, I pushed his ass towards me and begged him to fuck me even harder.

He quickened his pace and wrapped his arms around my tiny body. My legs trembled with every thrust of his massive cock as he hit my sweet spot with its head. He was building up the pressure inside my body, and if he continued, I was afraid I wouldn't be able to hold my orgasm back.

"Don't hold back," I groaned. "You can't break me."

He nodded with his eyes shut tight, and I could tell he was almost there, too. He drove into me even faster, holding me tighter under his huge body.

I arched my hips to meet his cock. I wanted so much of him, like he wanted me. His skin rubbed against my clit and sent enormous waves of pleasure all over my body. He panted even more above me as sweat trickled off his face and dropped to my cheeks.

He slammed his fist on the headboard, and I felt his cock tighten inside me.

"Oh, God, yes," I moaned. "Mine, mine."

Zarik roared as he shattered within me, his orgasm triggering my own, until we lay together, tangled and exhausted.

He held himself over me, supported by his elbows, as we panted.

I brushed my hair from my face. "You do know this is way too small for us to do this too often," I said breathlessly as I feebly waved my arm to indicate the room.

He nodded. "I agree. Want to go look for something that fits the both of us?"

I nodded as I kissed him, over and over.

Us.

Forever.

ZARIK

It was only yesterday that General Rouhr had bestowed the Silver Crystal on me and cleared up everything that I had obsessed about fixing.

Today, he was having a meeting in the town square for the entire city in order to fully explain what was happening with the Puppet Master and the planet.

I approved. By putting all of the information out there for everyone, maybe it would cut down on the anti-alien sentiment and help make things less volatile between all of us. Then again, even if I had not approved, I would be there anyway. I was assigned to guard duty.

A proper duty.

When I had gone to the armory to get the gear I needed for my guard work, the rest of the teams congratulated me and talked to me like I was one of their own.

Things were finally at a point where I was no longer the waste of space, but now someone of importance.

I took my position near the stage that had been erected in the square. The stage was very large, with over a dozen chairs set on it.

Sitting in the chairs were the women of our lives, a few city leaders, and the general. A light breeze blew from east to west through the square, bringing the tantalizing aromas of Lunch Lane to my nostrils. Something smelled good.

The large crowd that had already gathered were mumbling and getting to be a bit restless. I looked over at the stage to see Miri looking at me. I flashed her a smile, and was relieved to see the general rise from his seat and head towards the podium.

"My friends, people of Nyheim, and the people of Ankau watching this," he said with a nod to the cameras recording and broadcasting to the people unable to be here.

He opened up with a report about what we had found out in the woods; the lab, the synthetic memory-loss compound, the anti-alien group, all of it. While he spoke, several people in the crowd either gasped or called him a liar.

He took it all in stride, handling it with class. I

would have probably yelled back, called the hecklers all idiots, and had them forcefully removed in order to stop their stupidity from messing up my speech.

Then again, that's why I wasn't in charge and he was.

Between General Rouhr and Vidia, they explained everything about the Puppet Master and what was happening to the planet.

"PROVE IT!" someone in the crowd yelled out, immediately followed by numerous others demanding the same thing. I didn't like the look of the crowd. Too many of them were looking angry, skeptical, and far too nervous. Two men in particular were constantly whispering back and forth, pointing at the stage as they did. I motioned to one of the human guards and brought them to his attention.

"Keep an eye on them from where you are, I'll watch them from here," I whispered. He nodded.

"Very well," the general answered the crowd.

I glanced over and saw his face go blank for a second. "Ladies and gentlemen, I call for your calm and composed behavior. The being known as the Puppet Master will now send some of his tendrils up, not to attack, but to present himself and to communicate with us all."

Not a second later, dozens of tendrils slowly came out of the ground, sending several people on the outskirts of the crowd running away while many more screamed and yelled.

Things were getting out of hand as the tendrils erupted and snaked from the ground. After only a few seconds, things stopped. Four tendrils that came out by the stage wove their way towards a microphone that had been set up at the far corner. I had wondered why that was there.

But, how was the Puppet Master going to use electronics to speak to everyone? I thought he only spoke in our minds.

"There are times when I can do more than that, friend Zarik," came the answer. Okay, that was something different.

The tendrils wrapped themselves around the microphone and a little bit of feedback sounded through the speakers before the Puppet Master's unmistakable voice replaced it.

"I am the center of this world, and it is my charge, my duty, my responsibility to ensure that life on this world continues. I had no intention of causing harm, or causing any kind of pain and suffering when I first made my presence known."

He went on to explain that the Xathi ship crashing down on the planet and the subsequent leaking fuels and chemicals had awakened him. Those leaking chemicals, combined with the battles and the raping of resources by the humans were harming the planet, causing him to adjust what he did, which resulted in much of the vegetation of the planet suffering and dying.

Nothing like a giant talking plant to calm a crowd down.

Over the next hour, General Rouhr, Vidia, and the Puppet Master answered questions, accusations, and threats.

The threats were generally answered with an aimed rifle convincing them to stop, or a quick escort away.

I was diligent in my duties, watching the crowd, especially my two talkers. They weren't throwing out any threats or accusations, they were simply paying attention and talking between themselves.

The crowd was still a mixture of skepticism and fear, but it looked as though many in the square were starting to come around. They were believing us and starting to show trust in us. It was a relief to see.

Then it was time for the women to speak. Miri went first, and that had taken me by surprise. She quickly told her story, and I noticed that several people in the crowd ducked their heads in either shame or embarrassment, while some others seemed to be angry.

They looked to be angry at what happened, not that it was stopped. That was a good sign, there were people that were against the anti-alien groups.

The rest of the women spoke up, each telling their experiences and providing their expertise in regards to each particular situation they'd been involved in since we arrived. Finally, it was time for Jeneva to speak, and her words placed the final brick into the bridge that provided the way to unity and potential peace.

It didn't hurt that she had given birth to her and Vrehx's child a week ago and she had brought him with her. Skotan children were, well, if I was honest, we were ugly little things.

Our scales were constantly in flux, we already had some teeth, which made feeding something very painful from what I had heard.

We were terrible babies, ugly, and downright nasty.

It was a wonder anyone wanted to procreate.

However, I had seen this baby and by the cosmos, he was adorable. His scales were almost like feathers, light and soft little things on the surface of his skin. Tiny little red things, still almost transparent, over skin that matched Jeneva's skin tone.

No teeth, but a sweet smile when he slept, which was all the time. Skotan babies yelled and screamed all the time, this baby was quiet.

Jeneva's tale, as well as the presentation of her baby, swayed more people to our side than all of the other speeches combined.

Not even the Puppet Master was as convincing.

More questions were asked and answered, plans were made, and promises uttered to begin doing things the right way, to help rebuild everything properly.

We were no longer a divided populace—okay, we were, but not as badly divided—and were working on finding ways to work together.

We needed unity, not division.

The planet of Ankau was no longer a split planet.

It was now a planet that just happened to be home to several different peoples of different origins.

And I was proud to call it home.

EPILOGUE: MIRI

"Wow." I had said that word a few dozen times since the town meeting. I was still completely blown away from what was said, how people reacted, and from what I had seen from Jeneva.

A few hours ago, I had no clue who the woman was other than the first one to hook up with one of the aliens, and now as the first one to have a baby with one of them.

From what Zarik had told me, she had a few complications during the pregnancy, but she survived and now had a darling baby boy.

I had been lucky enough to sit only a few seats away from her and the baby, so I was able to see him.

Maybe obsess over him was a better phrase for it.

That idea that all babies are cute wasn't necessarily true. I had seen some not-so-cute babies.

I wouldn't call them ugly because no baby is ugly, but not all babies are the same in cuteness.

This baby, though, holy damn was that little dude cute as hell. The combination of human and Skotan DNA resulted in a very cute child. It helped that Jeneva was a babe and Vrehx was a decent-looking guy…I think.

I mean, I know that I'm in love with and highly attracted to a Skotan, but my Skotan looked better.

I looked up at him as we walked hand-in-hand, going to different parts of town looking for an apartment or something for us to live in.

His tiny little room wasn't exactly something that a couple could live in. I mean, it was *one* room, with nothing in it but a desk and a bed.

How could we live in a place that small?

And my apartment? Too many memories.

So, we were looking around, trying to find a quaint little place of our own. Maybe a place big enough for more than just the two of us.

Damn, that baby was friggin' cute.

I had apparently been staring at Zarik for a while. "Are you okay?" he asked me. "You've got a very weird look on your face."

"Oh," I said, shaking my head and turning away from him. "I was just thinking."

"I see," he smiled. "What about? As if I couldn't tell."

I stopped walking and looked at him. "What's that supposed to mean?"

He laughed. "You've had that look on your face ever since you saw Jeneva and the baby. I might not be terribly smart, but I can tell when you're thinking really hard about something."

I had to come clean. "Okay, okay. I am a little preoccupied right now. It's," I hesitated, "it's just that, I was wondering if you ever thought about," I took a breath and let it out slowly. He grabbed my hands and knelt down to look at me eye to eye. I smiled sheepishly, then continued. "Have you ever thought about having a family? You know, having kids and stuff?"

He smiled, kissed me on the cheek, then led me to a nearby bench. "To be honest, no."

Oh.

Well, that hurt. He put his hand on my chin and made me look at him. "At least not until now."

Wait, what?

He licked his lips and kept going. "I went through life thinking I would be a soldier forever. That we'd be fighting forever. I never thought that there would be time for me to be a father." He looked away for a moment and I could see the pain in his eyes. He was thinking about the mistake he had made so many years ago. "I wouldn't deserve to be a father."

I hoped for a "but" to be added to that. I *really* hoped for a "but".

He took a deep breath and turned back to me. "Then I met you and everything changed."

My heart started beating rapidly. My breath caught in my throat.

"Now, when I look at you," he said, "I can see my life being happy. I can see my life finally being worth living." He leaned in and kissed me. "And, mate, if you and I end up having children, I know that I would be the happiest male in the star system."

I let out a happy little squeal as I threw my arms around him and held him tightly. "Really? You mean it?"

I felt him nod against me and I couldn't have been happier. I was terrified at the idea of having a little life growing inside me, eventually, but the idea made me so happy.

Wait, *mate?* One thing at a time, brain.

"You have no idea how great that sounds to me," I said.

"I hope I do," he responded. "Because the idea of having children with you makes my heart race with joy." We kissed and I started to run my hands up and down his body. He gently pulled away from me and grabbed my hands. "Slow down. We're in public, remember?"

I actually hadn't, and that was a bit embarrassing. "Sorry."

"It's okay," he chuckled. "Maybe we should decide if we need a place for just the two of us, or something a little larger."

A little larger.

For a family.

Mate.

"Marry me," I blurted out.

He jerked his head back towards me, a mixture of shock and excitement in his eyes.

"What?"

I nodded. "Marry me. Like humans do. And we'll do whatever Skotan ritual you want." My mind raced. "There's so much I don't know, and you'll have to teach me, and..."

His face was blank.

Shit.

Maybe he hadn't meant to say mate yet. Maybe it was a slip of the tongue, or I'd misheard, or...

"You really want to be with me forever?" he asked, wonder in his voice.

I nodded, terrified.

Had I just taken it too far, too fast?

He lifted me until I was taller than even he was and swung me around, laughing.

"Whatever you want, whatever ceremony makes you happy," he said, and his smile shattered the fear around my throat.

"But what do you want?" I insisted.

"Miri," he said, "just stay by my side. That's all you need to do."

I smiled down on him and kissed him on the nose.

"Always."

LETTER FROM ELIN

And with that, we're starting to move into what my evil brain thinks of as phase three of the Conquered World...

Next we'll start to see the edges of a whole new enemy, one that even General Rouhr and the Urai never imagined.

And first up to meet the enemy?

Grumpy, snarky Sk'lar, the head of Strike team three. When he has to work with Phryne, the human head of security, you know sparks are going to fly!

Keep reading for a sneak peek of Sk'lar!

XOXO,

Elin

SK'LAR: SNEAK PEEK

P hryne

The blaring alarm startled me so badly that I jumped. Scalding hot coffee splashed over the steel rim of my cup and onto the array of datapads on my desk.

"Shit," I muttered more out of frustration rather than fear. I'd woken up hours before my alarm was set to go off. I'd been doing that ever since our sky split open and genocidal bug aliens started pouring into our world.

That was over a year ago, yet I still couldn't manage to remember to turn off my alarm.

I grabbed a cloth and dabbed coffee off the surface of the datapads. I'd spent the better part of two hours reading over various reports from the city of Nyhiem and nearly every surrounding settlement.

Three days ago, General Rouhr and Councilwoman Vidia – my boss- decided to make an ally of the giant tentacle-y plant thing that held us hostage not too long ago.

It's sentient enough to hold a conversation, which was a huge surprise to me. However, I hadn't had the opportunity to converse with it myself.

Honestly, I wasn't sure if I wanted to.

A week ago, I was brainstorming ideas on how to kill the damn thing. Vidia and Rouhr might've been able to switch gears and take their tea with the thing but I wasn't ready to do that. After all, the plant thing was smart enough to use advanced military tactics.

I should start calling it by its name, I supposed. The Puppet Master. Not sure who came up with that. It was clever when the thing was our enemy. It seemed a little rude now that the creature was our ally, but politeness wasn't one of my strong suits. I was too direct for that kind of thing.

I get results.

Sometimes I have to be kind of a dick those results but I didn't lose any sleep over it.

The reports I'd been reading mostly consisted of various groups bitching about General Rouhr and Vidia's decision to accept the Puppet Master as an ally.

I could understand their hesitation. The average citizen wasn't privy to the details exchanged between their leader and the Puppet Master in that hole in the desert.

I, however, was privy to those details. In fact, I had that conversation and all others following carefully transcribed and sent over to me. That was what was on one of the many datapads strewn across my workspace.

Once the spilled coffee was wiped up, I got up to get ready for my day. I'd gotten a fair amount of work done but nowhere near as much as I wanted to have done by now.

Vidia often said that was one of my downfalls. I could do ten times the work of everyone else and still think I haven't done enough.

I walked to my bathroom. My apartment complex was right next to the central government building of Nyhiem. It came complimentary with the job.

Damn good thing it did, too. My home was destroyed during the Xathi invasion.

I knew that didn't make me special.

Plenty of other people lost so much more than just their home. In fact, my apartment was so nice in comparison to all of the emergency housing that I often felt guilty.

Whole families were crammed into an apartment the size of a shoebox. Here I was in my studio with my bathroom that bordered on luxurious in comparison to others.

Three people could fit in my shower. I consistently had hot water, a luxury many often went without.

As guilty as I felt for having things so many didn't, I knew I'd earned these rewards. Even before aliens invaded my world I worked hard. Harder than anyone. It took years for me to get where I was now.

My first job after leaving the orphanage where I spent my childhood was an assistant to the security department in Fraga. Now, I was the security department.

Everything went through me, at least where the humans were concerned. I didn't have authority over General Rouhr's aliens. That was something that irked me but was simultaneously a relief.

Over the past few months, I'd gotten plenty of opportunities to work with the Skotan, K'ver, and Valorni soldiers. They were far more advanced than any human soldier could ever hope to be. They had better weapons and first-rate training.

However, even the mildest of our alien allies had an element of unpredictability that would not be fun to control. I didn't envy General Rouhr when it came to that aspect of his job. No wonder he always looked somewhat disgruntled.

As I scrubbed my hair and skin with a bar of standard-issue soap that smelled like wax, I went over what I had to get done today.

Vidia wanted to do a press conference of some kind soon. I didn't think it was a good idea. Not yet.

Things were still too volatile among the people. As of right now, the aliens were tolerated by their respective communities. Some people welcomed them with open arms. Some people were practically frothing at the mouth to expel all aliens from the planet.

Vidia wasn't overly concerned with those people. She believed the anti-alien factions to be very small and spread out.

However, based on reports I'd been reading over the last two days, I had reason to suspect the anti-alien mindset was more widespread than Vidia thought.

Then there was the matter of the Puppet Master. How was I supposed to work something like that creature into my security protocols? It's not like I could fingerprint it and have it scanned into the systems. Naturally, the Puppet Master's strengths would be in the defense department. Or as a spy. It still amazed me that something so big stayed hidden for so long.

My water pressure flickered, jarring me out of my thoughts. I'd been in the shower for too long. I was going to fall behind if I didn't pick up the pace.

I stepped out of the shower, dried off and pulled on my work clothes for the day. I technically didn't have a uniform but I wore the same dark, close fit pants and the same tactical shirt in different colors most days.

Today, I chose a thunder cloud grey shirt.

Before I left my apartment, I caught a glimpse of myself in the mirror.

My chin length red hair was still wet. Hopefully, it would dry nicely. I didn't spend hours primping in front of a mirror but that didn't mean I wanted to look like a ragamuffin.

Lack of sleep had made my complexion look a little wan as of late but only I would notice something like that about myself. Light bounced off my sharp cheekbones making me look more angular than I really was.

I always thought my blue eyes were a little too big for my face but that came in handy when I wanted to shoot someone down with a withering stare.

Overall, I looked fine enough for work.

The walk to the central building was quick. I hadn't made it to the elevators before two human males stepped up to me.

"Good morning ma'am," the first said.

"Is there anything we should know for the briefing today?" The second asked.

I gave them a blank look. I had no idea who these

two were.

"Are you trainees?" I asked.

"No," the first said slowly. The second tried to subtly roll his eyes but I caught the movement. "I'm Tona. This is Skit."

They said it like their names should mean something to me.

"We've met several times."

"I meet people every day," I replied.

"General Rouhr assigned us to your team after our work with the hybrid outbreak?" The other one, Skit, prompted.

"Oh." A tight smile spread across my lips. "I remember now. It's hard to forget the two guards injected into my squad without my approval or even my permission."

My squad was hand selected to my specifications. It took the better part of a year to assemble my elite team. I was very selective. The interview process was extremely thorough.

"With all due respect, ma'am. We're more than a pair of frontier guards. We wouldn't be here if General Rouhr didn't think we deserved it," Tona said.

"Be that as it may," I pressed, "General Rouhr isn't your boss. You're on my squad which makes me your boss. The only thing that matters now is that you do your job to my standard, not General Rouhr's. Are we understood?"

Tona and Skit saluted to show their understanding.

"Good boys."

I moved passed them and entered the elevator. The doors closed before the two of them could step onto the lift. I relished the final moments of silence before my work day truly began. There was a briefing in a few hours.

I still had a few details I wanted to smooth over.

I was planning on bringing up the anti-alien factions. New construction projects were popping up all over the settled land. Each project would need its own security detail.

We've already learned that anti-alien radicals had no issue disrupting construction projects.

That little nugget of logic was lost on me.

Why target efforts that would make life better for fellow humans?

Some of General Rouhr's best soldiers were scheduled to be in the briefing today. Some of them spent a lot of time in the field lately.

Perhaps, they would offer insight into the behavior of the anti-alien group. Assuming any of the radicals were ballsy enough to openly harass a group of General Rouhr's soldiers, that is.

The anti-alien radicals we'd interacted with thus far

were that ballsy but also very stupid. It stood to reason that future factions would be less foolhardy especially since we were cracking down on punishments.

Whatever the case, this briefing was sure to be an interesting one.

Sk'lar

The cargo ship's engines hummed merrily as we gained altitude in the clear blue sky. From my position in front of the windscreen of the atmosphere bound ship, I could see the uneven skyline of Amarita spread out in the distance on the shores of the crawling sea.

"Approaching Amarita proper on vector 201x."

I turned to regard the corporal piloting our craft. He

was a K'ver, just as I was. Jet black skin rippled with muscle in his toned forearms, emblazoned with hair thin silver circuitry. Since he's low rank, he only had the most basic implants.

As a ranking officer, I had many more. For example, an implant near the back of my brain increased the flow of neurons between my nervous and muscular systems, meaning I could stand steady even when our craft encountered the stiff wind blowing off the coast.

"Minor turbulence, sir. Compensating."

"Hold her steady, Corporal. The last thing we need is to crash on top of a human dwelling and stir up more xenophobia."

"Yes, sir." The corporal's hands flashed over the controls, and soon the chassis stopped shaking. He glanced at me, black eyes inscrutable. "Sir, If I may pose a question?"

"I believe you just did, Corporal, but go ahead."

"Yes sir. Hasn't the anti-alien sentiment mostly run its course by now? I mean, after the whole mind-wiping fiasco."

"You keep a close eye on current events, I see." I nodded in approval. "Yes, their movement has definitely taken a hit, and many humans have rejected them. However, if there's one thing that my admittedly shallow perusal of human history tells me, many of their species don't behave rationally. There was one orange skinned fellow in the early twenty first century who—"

A light flashed on the console, and the Corporal quickly scanned a read out.

"Report?"

"Sir, sensors are picking up some sort of structures near the Vengeance Crater. It looks like the start of a settlement or colony."

My lips grew tight on my face. I walked over to sit down at one of the monitoring stations.

"Patch in the feed to my screen, Corporal."

"Yes, sir."

The monitor flashed briefly, then depicted a series of crudely constructed buildings surrounded by a perimeter fence. I held my chin in my hand as I took in the sight of some salvaged atmospheric transports which had been modified with weaponry.

The compound seemed to be abuzz with activity, and I quickly lost count of how many bodies were milling about in the throng.

"Corporal, get me an estimate on the number of life signs within that compound."

"Yes, sir." His fingers whiz across the console, making adjustments even as he continued to keep our flight steady. "It appears that I can't give you an accurate estimate. The compound has jamming technology. I can only scan those life forms outside of its walls."

I already knew the answer before I asked my next question, but I had to verify my intuition.

"What's the racial breakdown of the life forms you can scan, Corporal?"

He fiddled with the console for a bit, then turned his head around to regard me with a grim expression.

"All human, sir."

"I see." Silently observing the compound as I pondered what our move should be, I felt a certain trepidation build within me. These were the kinds of decisions I was supposed to make as a Team Commander.

But I couldn't help but feel like I was out of my element. I knew I was a capable soldier, and my implants put me in the league of the other races. I couldn't arm wrestle a Valorni, perhaps, but I would bet on myself in a fisticuffs none the less.

However, I had limited experience with command positions. In many ways, I wondered if I wasn't appointed the head of Team Three just because of convenience, and not because I was the best candidate for the job.

Here I stood, for good or ill, and the corporal was waiting for me to make a decision. We should just finish the supply run, but the compound hadn't been on any briefings that had been disclosed to me. I couldn't pass up the opportunity to garner new information on what could be a potential threat to peace.

"Take us down, Corporal."

"Sir?" He couldn't quite hide a note of fear in his tone. I couldn't blame him. The last thing I wanted to do was land in a nest of hostile humans.

The potential gains outweighed the risks, though.

"You have your orders."

"Understood, sir."

"But try to bring us down near the southern gate. Most of their vehicles and munitions seems to be concentrated to the north east. If they want to get… testy…we'll be in a good position to flee."

"Yes, sir."

The corporal took us into a shallow dive into the blasted, melted rock canyon where the *Vengeance* once stood. Now there was nothing left but a crater of that mighty vessel, and if that was not a warning to be cautious I didn't know what was.

We dipped down below the level of the compound. Multicolored strata flashed past the viewing port as we skimmed just beneath the surface of the crater.

I doubted they had any weaponry trained on the crater itself, but apprehension still threatened to overwhelm me. At any moment our unshielded peaceful vessel might be perforated by munitions fire from hostile humans.

I knew I shouldn't make assumptions. Just because this was an unregistered settlement of pure strain humans didn't automatically make them hostile.

But I had learned as a warrior that it was not just your brain that you must rely on, but your instinct. The humans called it 'going with your gut,' which was about as silly a notion as I could imagine, but now in the moment I believed I was beginning to understand its meaning.

The corporal nosed the ship up and we flashed above the crater's edge. It was obvious that our arrival had not gone unnoticed. A large group of humans were clustered about the southern gate, and even from this distance they didn't seem all that friendly.

"I guess this is the Welcome Wagon."

"Sir?" The corporal's brow wrinkled in confusion.

"It's a human expression. I was being sarcastic. I think we'd best prepare for antagonism from these creatures."

"Agreed."

The corporal set our craft down about thirty meters away from the gate. Our landing pylons had barely extended into the grassy turf when the gate opened and the mob of humanity came spilling out.

They weren't charging our position, but they walked

with a menacing purpose that made me second guess my decision to investigate.

"Keep her hot and ready to lift off," I clapped my hand on his shoulder. My old CO used to do that, and it oddly helped calm my nerves.

"Yes, sir."

My boots clanked off the metal deck plating as I went down into the cargo bay. Because this was a peaceful supply run, I didn't have the entirety of Team Three with me. However, protocol insisted that I bring at least three along even on an ostensibly peaceful mission.

The biggest member of my crew was Tyehn. A big burly Valorni, he had to cut the sleeves off his skin suit to accommodate his size.

I silently considered if I should speak to someone about him; I swore he kept getting bigger each time I saw him. Tyehn held his salute crisply, perhaps because his laughter had been the most boisterous when I came below deck.

Jalok stood two inches shorter than Tyehn, but one look at his stone cold expression and you realized that he was the one you should be afraid of.

Jalok was an expert at close quarters combat, though he was pretty accurate with munitions as well, and those Skotan scales were a nice addition.

Finally, Cazak gave me his version of a salute, which

was limp and casual. He wasn't the most intimidating being in a fight, but he had a true knack for repairing and maintaining field equipment. Cazak was the only member of my team I requested by name, but to be honest it wasn't hard to get him. His attitude rubbed a lot of commanders the wrong way, to use a human phrase.

"At ease." They relaxed somewhat, and Cazak gave me a little smirk I chose to ignore, even though it hit me right in the confidence. "As I'm sure you've noticed, we've made an unscheduled landing. There's a human settlement that's not supposed to be here, and we are going to make contact."

"Finally, some action." Tyehn reached for a two-handed pulse rifle but I held up my hand and shook my head.

"Not so fast. You're a bit too threatening in appearance. Head up front and assist our pilot in any way he wishes."

His face crinkled with disappointment.

"But he's only a corporal."

"In any way he wishes, Tyehn."

"Yes, sir."

With a sigh of resignation, he headed up to the front. I turned my attention to the other two.

"Small side arms only. We don't want to alarm them."

With Jalok and Cazak in tow, I pressed the panel which lowered the exit ramp. The crowd of humans had gathered a short distance away. When they first caught sight of us in our skin suits, they started booing.

Jalok tensed up next to me. I whispered surreptitiously in his ear.

"Easy, Jalok. We're not here to fight."

"Try telling that to *them*." Still, his fingers uncurled from around the hilt of his side arm.

I approached the throng with purpose, refusing to show any sign of weakness while still trying to appear non-threatening.

An older human male stepped forward, a slapdash projectile weapon clutched in one hand. At least the barrels were pointed at the ground—for now.

"Salutations." I offered a small bow of my head, and my soldiers followed suit. "I am Commander Sk'lar of the K'ver Central Command," a small lie. "Who speaks for you?"

In response, one of the humans spat a wad of white froth at my feet. Jalok's eyes narrowed, but he holds his place.

The older human grinned at the display and stepped right up in front of me.

"I speak for us. And if you can't tell, you obsidian skinned droid spawn aren't welcome here."

"We come in peace. Your settlement isn't registered

and we were simply investigating if you needed any assistance."

A young child shouted out from the throng. "You can assist by going the hell away."

A ripple of laughter rose into the warm air.

"We don't need anything from a bunch of aliens. Now beat it, and tell the rest of your inky brethren not to come back."

"Humans are not native to this planet." I grimaced at Cazak's smarmy grin. "That kind of makes us ALL aliens here."

The sound of weapons powering up in the crowd had me thinking this could go bad fast. Ignoring Cazak, I bowed my head to the lead human.

"Then we go in peace."

I turned on my heel and walk back toward the ship, Cazak and Jalok falling in behind me. As soon as our backs are turned a wave of open threats and insults were hurled at us.

A soft bodied fruit smashed between my shoulder blades, setting juice running down my skinsuit, but I didn't even slow my stride.

"Sir?" Jalok looked at me with widened eyes, as if unbelieving that I didn't react to the hurled vegetation.

"As you are, Jalok." We got back inside the ship and the ramp raised up flush with the hull. I relayed the order to the pilot to take us up post haste.

As our craft climbed back into the sky, my mind was troubled. I had a feeling that this settlement was going to be a thorn in the side of anyone who wanted peace between the races.

Phryne

I frowned and checked the time on my wrist device for the third time since the briefing was supposed to officially start. Twenty minutes passed and there was no sign of General Rouhr's soldiers.

Personally, I didn't think we needed to wait for them. All meetings were carefully documented. The soldiers could catch themselves up whenever they deigned to make an appearance.

"Should we send a search unit?" Vidia reached over to General Rouhr, who sat beside her, and squeezed his forearm. Concern flooded her expression. I tried not to frown.

Vidia and General Rouhr made a great team. They worked well together politically, socially, and on every other level that mattered and quite a few that didn't. However, I never approved of allowing emotions to show through in a professional setting. There was a job to do. Becoming consumed with fear or worry wasn't going to help get that job done.

"Do you think something's gone wrong?" I asked.

"None of the team I sent out is answering their comms." General Rouhr's frown remained prominently on his face. "Vidia's right. Let's send a small search fleet to their last location."

General Rouhr was about to send the order when a brilliant pale blue light appeared in the room.

"Oh, hell no," I muttered.

Rift travel was a wonderful innovation that was slowly integrating itself into everyday operations. It was wildly convenient if not uncomfortable to utilize.

However, it was meant to be impossible to walk through a rift into high-security areas like this one without going through the proper clearance procedures.

I knew the proper procedures hadn't been performed in this case because I was the person who approved the damn requests. I locked eyes with Vidia who looked apologetic.

Yes, she technically was my boss but she knew how I was about this sort of thing. Control was key, especially in a tumultuous time such as this.

I reached for the weapon strapped to my side in case it was indeed a threat coming through a rift into our base of operations. I was ready to pull it loose and fire right up until a dark bald head appeared in the blue light.

A K'ver stepped through the rift portal. His expression was gravely serious. I took my hand off my weapon.

Naturally, it would've been a K'ver that circumvented the security protocols. I eyed the glowing lines of complex circuitry that lined his arms and the left side of his neck.

The light of the rift portal faded back into nothing and I was able to get a good look at the K'ver. His strong jaw was clenched. There was a somber expression in his solid obsidian eyes.

Something strange flickered in my chest.

My anger dimmed.

Something about this K'ver, though I couldn't put my finger on it, reminded me of an old childhood friend from the orphanage.

I shook the thought away. Now wasn't the time.

"Apologies for disregarding protocol," the K'ver said to me.

Clearly, he knew who I was meaning we must've met at one point or another. Perhaps this was what Vidia meant when she said I needed to work on my interpersonal relationships.

"I expect you to tell me why you did so." I lifted my chin and gave him a stern look. With the other aliens, the Valorni especially, it was important to physically demonstrate a lack of intimidation. Ordinarily, that wasn't a problem for me but suddenly thinking of my time at the orphanage threw me off.

"Of course," he nodded. "General Rouhr," the K'ver turned away from me to address his general. "Our recon team was attacked at the old *Vengeance* landing site."

Even now, General Rouhr's face darkened with a shadow of sadness. Vidia gave his forearm another squeeze. I didn't understand the love the general had for his vessel, but then again, I'd never been assigned on a ship. Regardless, the loss of the *Vengeance* deeply affected the General.

"What happened, Sk'lar?" General Rouhr inquired, the sadness gone as quickly as it appeared.

"Anti-alien fanatics," the K'ver, Sk'lar, said with a dismissive shake of his head. "No injuries but considerable threats."

"Do you think there's any substance to those threats?" I asked.

"Potentially," Sk'lar nodded. "This group was more organized than others we've dealt with in the past. I wouldn't take anything they say too lightly."

"I expect a full report detailing the exact words exchanged," I said.

Sk'lar tapped a device strapped to his wrist that connected right into the circuits on his skin.

"Not a problem."

"Good." I nod curtly.

"I'd like that report sent to me as well," General Rouhr asked. Sk'lar nodded.

At that moment, a Valorni came through the door out of breath and covered in a light sheen of sweat.

"I came as soon as I could," he panted. I'd met this one before too but his name escaped me.

"Karzin, what took you so long?" The hint of a smirk appeared on Sk'lar's mouth.

"I went through the proper channels," Karzin grumbled.

"Which is appreciated," I tossed in.

"Did you tell her about the anti-alien jackasses?" Karzin asked Sk'lar.

"You're picking up the local lingo nicely, Karzin," General Rouhr interjected. "Yes, we've been briefed on the situation."

"What are we going to do about it?" Karzin demanded.

"We should focus on preventative measures," Skit jumped in. "Completely suppressing them will only cause a stronger uprising."

I lifted a brow. Solid logic. Not bad, kid.

"Declaw them instead of exterminate them," Vidia said thoughtfully.

"They'll likely start acting out more as soon as election campaigns are underway," I said. "Vidia, you're the favorite among much of the population but anti-alien groups aren't going to want you in a position of power."

Vidia, the former mayor of Fraga, ran Nyhiem while our world rebuilt itself after the Xathi attack. During the crisis and its aftermath, Vidia took the helm of leadership.

At the end of the Xathi war, the council invited her to carry on mayoral duties during the rebuilding period. She did so faithfully, rebuilding the city until it was ready for elections.

Now that things had quieted down, other prominent people from the Pre-Xathi government wanted to go back to an electoral system.

Personally, I wished they'd leave it alone. Vidia had done a remarkable job keeping the planet on its feet after the Xathi invasion. She's clearly the best for the job which is why I wasn't worried about her ability to prove it in an election.

However, I was worried about her safety especially with all these anti-alien capsules popping up everywhere. I'd feel better if I had a headcount.

"I want you two in the streets," I said to Tona and Skit. "I want you in civilian clothes. Talk to anyone and everyone about the anti-alien bullshit. Keep a recording device and your GPS on at all times. I give you creative freedom but we need an idea of how prominent these groups are within the city."

"Yes ma'am," Skit nodded.

"Where are we with the food inventory?" General Rouhr asked.

Tona grabbed a datapad and pulled up a report.

"Our numbers are steadily improving," he informed us.

"There sounds like there's a 'but' at the end of that." Vidia smiled sadly.

"The Xathi destroyed so much. Valuable, fertile lands were destroyed and will take time to replenish. The land we can use is in good shape and the output is in the top percentile but we won't be off rations by the end of the year like we hoped."

"Anything we can do to boost crop output?" General Rouhr asked.

"Not without using harmful agents."

"Can't do that," General Rouhr frowned. "The Puppet Master would be most displeased with us."

"Could we ask its permission?"

"If someone walked up to you and asked if they could pour acid on your arm, would you agree to it?" Vidia prompted.

"Point taken."

"What about the construction of new settlements?" General Rouhr moved on.

"The eco-construction is going very well," Tona reported. "That Puppet Master thing is an architectural genius."

"The fruits of the alliance are already showing," General Rouhr grinned.

"We could use that for the election," I spoke up. "Vidia played an active role in forming our liaison with the Puppet Master and there's a clear link to a positive output."

"What matters is that the work gets done, not that I keep my power," Vidia said kindly.

"Having you in power is what's allowing the work to get done," I corrected. "It's in the best interest of everyone that you officially take the reins of the Capital and keep our progress as a planet flourishing."

"If you weren't so damn brilliant with the security team, I'd have you writing my speeches," Vidia joked.

"I don't think I have the interpersonal skills for that." Vidia was one of the few people I openly joked with. I had a skill for keeping my professional life and work like separated but I considered Vidia a friend.

"Fair enough," Vidia chuckled. "Besides, I'd rather have you there to keep me alive."

"Which is something we should discuss in further detail." I steered the conversation back to the issues at hand. "I'm confident Skit and Tona will find evidence of anti-alien factions growing bolder within the city as well as within the settlements. I want to impose extra security measures here so we're prepared."

"What do you suggest?" Vidia asked.

"One of the trends I've noticed is that no matter how rowdy an anti-alien faction member is, they're hesitant to directly engage in combat. Correct?" I looked to Sk'lar for confirmation. He nodded.

"The anti-alien radicals understand that they are physically outmatched against General Rouhr's forces. We should allocate a defense team specifically for Vidia during the election period," I suggested.

"I think that's an excellent idea," General Rouhr agreed. "Sk'lar, what do you have your team working on lately?"

Sk'lar hesitated which I found surprising. He didn't look like the type to hesitate.

"Routine patrols focusing on the old *Vengeance* site and the Aurora, sir," Sk'lar replied.

"I'm going to reassign your strike team. You'll be

working with Phryne to ensure Vidia's safety at all times."

"Yes, sir."

GET SK'LAR NOW!

https://elinwynbooks.com/conquered-world-alien-romance/

PLEASE DON'T FORGET TO LEAVE A REVIEW!

Readers rely on your opinions, and your review can help others decide on what books they read. Make sure your opinion is heard and leave a review where you purchased this book!

Don't miss a new release! You can sign up for release alerts at both Amazon and Bookbub:
    bookbub.com/authors/elin-wyn
    amazon.com/author/elinwyn

For a free short story, opportunities for advance review copies, release news and the occasional cat picture, please join the newsletter!
    https://elinwynbooks.com/newsletter-signup/

And don't forget the Facebook group, where I post sneak peeks of chapters and covers!
https://www.facebook.com/groups/ElinWyn/

DON'T MISS THE STAR BREED!

Given: Star Breed Book One

When a renegade thief and a genetically enhanced mercenary collide, space gets a whole lot hotter!

Thief Kara Shimsi has learned three lessons well - keep her head down, her fingers light, and her tithes to the syndicate paid on time.

But now a failed heist has earned her a death sentence - a one-way ticket to the toxic Waste outside the dome. Her only chance is a deal with the syndicate's most ruthless enforcer, a wolfish mountain of genetically-modified muscle named Davien.

The thought makes her body tingle with dread-or is it heat?

Mercenary Davien has one focus: do whatever is necessary to get the credits to get off this backwater mining colony and back into space. The last thing he wants is a smart-mouthed thief - even if she does have the clue he needs to hunt down whoever attacked the floating lab he and his created brothers called home.

Caring is a liability. Desire is a commodity. And love could get you killed.

https://elinwynbooks.com/star-breed/

ABOUT THE AUTHOR

I love old movies – *To Catch a Thief, Notorious, All About Eve* — and anything with Katherine Hepburn in it. Clever, elegant people doing clever, elegant things.

I'm a hopeless romantic.

And I love science fiction and the promise of space.

So it makes perfect sense to me to try to merge all of those loves into a new science fiction world, where dashing heroes and lovely ladies have adventures, get into trouble, and find their true love in the stars!

www.ingramcontent.com/pod-product-compliance
Lightning Source LLC
Chambersburg PA
CBHW070737180626
46818CB00007B/2885

* 9 7 8 1 9 4 0 9 2 4 6 1 8 *